THE BOUNTY KILLERS

Most bounty hunters operated legally to bring their quarries to justice 'dead or alive'. But for Big Jack Corrigan however, it had to be dead every time — and the law took objection to that. So, to prevent bounty hunters killing the killers, deputy US Marshal Lee Saleen followed when Corrigan and his henchmen set off in pursuit of bank robber and killer Pearly Gillis and his gang. Surrounded by enemies, how would Saleen cope against the overwhelming odds?

12

14

OWEN G. IRONS

THE BOUNTY KILLERS

Complete and Unabridged

LINFORD
Leicester

First published in Great Britain in 2007 by
Robert Hale Limited
London

First Linford Edition
published 2009
by arrangement with
Robert Hale Limited
London

British Library CIP Data

Irons, Owen G.
  The bounty killers.—Large print ed.—
Linford western library
  1. Western stories
  2. Large type books
  I. Title
  823.9'14 [F]

  ISBN 978–1–84782–546–9

Published by
F. A. Thorpe (Publishing)
Anstey, Leicestershire

Set by Words & Graphics Ltd.
Anstey, Leicestershire
Printed and bound in Great Britain by
T. J. International Ltd., Padstow, Cornwall

This book is printed on acid-free paper

1

It wasn't much of a bank as banks go. Adobe bricks supported a flat plank roof. The front door was thick, but hardly intimidating. A good mule kick would have brought the whole structure down. The problem, of course, was the steel safe inside. Even that troubled the robbers only a little.

In a few minutes the bank manager would be arriving. He would open the safe for them. There is little a man won't do to co-operate when he has the muzzle of a Colt revolver nudging the back of his head.

The three men waited. It was cool in the inky shadows of morning. Seen by any passerby, Charley Stoddard would have seemed almost indifferent to the proceedings. The lanky robber sat against the night-chilled earth, his bony knees thrust up. The thin man had a bit of straw between his lips. He held the reins to his long-legged gray horse loosely with one hand and traced meaningless figures in the sandy soil with the other. His hat was tugged low, his demeanor deceptive. He was not indifferent, only vastly patient.

Billy Gillis offered a far different impression. The youngest of the three men by far, he was perspiring in the cool of morning. Each passing rider or wagon, no matter how innocuous, caused fear to surge through his body. He had hung his battered Stetson on the pommel of his dun horse's saddle and now and then ran his stubby fingers through his curly dark hair like a man in extreme agitation. This was far from being the twenty-year-old's first crime, but it was the most daring and brazen he had attempted.

The leader of the group was Pearly Gillis, Billy's much older cousin. Pearly had already robbed three banks across western New Mexico since his release from Yuma prison where he had done seven years for manslaughter, avoiding the noose only because his jury had been unable to decide who had drawn first in the brawl at Casa Grande. Pearly had not since killed anyone to Billy's knowledge, but in the deep-set eyes of the hawk-faced man one could always see the devil dancing.

Just now Pearly Gillis stood at the head of the alley studying the length of Adobe Falls's main street, its clutter of ill-built stores, saloons and stables, as coolly as if he were waiting to meet a friend, not like someone who was preparing to rob a bank.

'I think this is our man,' Pearly told the others without turning his head.

Charley Stoddard was to his feet as quickly as a cat, shifting the twin holsters he wore to a more purposeful angle. Billy's heart, which had been racing before, now rose to a trip-hammer rhythm. He watched his cousin with commingled dread and admiration. Pearly had no nerves at all, it had been said. The longer they rode together, the nearer Billy came to believing it. Strongly put together, sun-darkened and cool, Pearly was everything Billy wished to emulate. Yet he hadn't the 'stuff' his cousin possessed. Billy regretted having fallen in with Pearly now, but now it was too late.

'It's him,' Pearly said coldly, taking the reins to his leggy Appaloosa from Stoddard without glancing at him. Pearly Gillis's focus was on the slightly rotund man in a blue pin-striped suit, town shoes and derby hat making his way toward the front of the bank, fishing out his key chain from his trousers-pocket.

'We'll walk the horses over,' Pearly said, reminding them of their plan. 'Billy, you hold them outside. This won't take long.'

Moving through the pooled shadows of early morning, Billy glanced up at the raw, jumbled form of the lower Rocky Mountain slopes thrusting into the bright blue skies beyond the outskirts of Adobe Falls. His fear deepened with each step he took as they crossed the dusty street, Pearly timing their advance to coincide with the manager's arrival at the bank's green door. Pearly showed no fear, no anxiety of any sort. Maybe his long years on the run, in prison, in myriad gunfights had inured him to such trivial concerns. Pearly had told Bill that he expected to meet his Maker in a hail of gunfire one day. Maybe that sort of fatalism steels a man.

Billy did not want to go down like that. At twenty he expected to live for ever. Pearly had chatted up a few of the local residents in a barrel-head saloon and had become convinced that the town marshal, a man named Pollack, was not daring by nature, and would be unlikely to pursue any criminal beyond his jurisdiction. The county sheriff was located far away in Santa Fe. By the time he was even advised of the robbery, the Gillises and Charley Stoddard would have made Texas or perhaps Mexico, their saddle-bags filled with stolen gold.

The round man with the keys to the bank glanced up once from under the brim of his derby, apparently saw nothing to make him wary as Pearly approached him along the boardwalk, inserted the key into the bank's door and turned the knob. Billy saw Pearly thrust his boot into the door's opening, saw him hiss something into the banker's ear and saw him prod the little man with the barrel of his Colt Peacemaker.

Pearly Gillis's movements were abrupt but smooth. The banker saw Pearly's boot holding the door open, felt the rough jab of the pistol in his ribs, heard the bandit's coolly spoken threat, 'Open up or die here', and complied. The little man drew up enough courage from his internal resources as they entered the bank to splutter:

'What's this all about?' but he already knew.

'Open the safe,' Pearly ordered in his

controlled voice.

'I will not!' the banker said despite the threat of the blue-steel Colt in the gunman's hand. Pearly slammed his fist into the banker's face, sending the pudgy little man reeling back against the wall.

'I don't have the time to play with you,' Pearly Gillis said with true menace. The muzzle of his revolver lowered slightly. 'I'll shoot your kneecap off, and if that doesn't convince you, I'll shoot the other one. You've five seconds to decide how you want this to go.'

The banker was not a coward, neither was he a fool. He knew that Pearly meant what he was saying. The dark, Apache features of the bandit made that clear. The prospect of spending the rest of his years as a cripple made the decision for him. Shakily the banker made his way to the green safe with its flourishes of gold curlicues.

Outside Charley Stoddard lounged against the wall near the bank's door. The green shade on the windows remained down, the CLOSED sign was still displayed. A local man, a sodbuster from the look of him, glanced at his watch, at the bank, shook his head and walked away.

Young Billy Gillis watched the mute-play with surging anxiety. He tried to calm the horses who seemed to sense his unease. He looked to the skies where a rising sun colored the spectacular mountain range with deep violet and crimson. Adobe Falls was awakening now. A shopkeeper was sweeping his section of the boardwalk opposite. A few cowboys, tired but happy with their previous night's celebration, straggled down the street on their ponies.

The gunshot from within the bank creased the silence of the early morning and Billy's head jerked around to see Pearly dashing from the bank, saddlebags in his hand. Pearly tossed the pouches and their contents to Charley Stoddard who, once ignited, moved like a wind-driven brushfire.

There was no wasted motion as the

lanky gunman caught the saddle-bags, secured them and swung into leather.

Billy moaned inwardly and shoved a shaky boot into his stirrup. Then, together, the three robbers spurred their mounts down the dusty gray street of Adobe Falls and out into the open country beyond, followed by three or four shots from some alert citizen's Winchester. None of these bullets came near to tagging them and within minutes they were out on to the broad red-rock country, riding free. By the time any townspeople could awake, rub their eyes, rush to their horses and saddle them, the outlaws would be lost in the vastness of the New Mexico desert.

'What happened, then?' Charley Stoddard asked Pearly as the three outlaws slowed their ponies, not wanting to run them into the ground.

'Little bastard had a pistol inside the safe,' Pearly answered.

Charley only nodded knowingly. Young Billy Gillis began to feel guilty, sick and doomed. Bank robbery was bad enough, but Pearly now had them on the run for murder.

An hour later the sun was still low and faintly colored as they crossed the vast expanse of sandy desert, littered here and there with black volcanic rock. The mesas to the north were a low line of dark land galleons looming against the crystal sky. Foothills lay ahead, desolate and stark, touched with the green of growth only at their lowest reaches. Billy glanced back constantly and although he saw nothing, no one, his anxiety continued to ride with him.

'Aren't we go to turn south?' he asked.

Pearly shook his head. Now trail-dusty, streaked with perspiration, his face was grim. 'No, Billy. We're bound for Arizona Territory.'

'But I thought . . . '

Pearly laughed harshly. 'I just spread the word around that I was bound for Texas to throw off any of those rubes who might consider looking for us after they heard about the bank robbery. Remember that, Billy,' Pearly said, fixing his dark eyes on his cousin's. 'Don't tell anyone the truth if you want to survive. A few lies can buy you miles — and years.'

They rode on in silence, their horses now settled into a walk as noon came and went. Although Billy knew that they could not ride the animals hard and long out on the empty desert, still his heart fought against this logic with spurring fear. He wanted to ride fast and hard, as far from Adobe Falls as his dun could carry him.

'I guess we should lay up at the springs for awhile,' the laconic Charley Stoddard commented after they had traveled another few miles. 'The horses can use some rest. There's no other water until we reach Camden Creek.'

Pearly Gillis only nodded. That had been his intention all along. Lay up at Bullhead Springs, unsaddle the horses, let them drink their fill and wait until the desert sun had lowered its head in

11

the west. The flat landscape behind them would afford them plenty of warning if anyone was attempting to track them. That now seemed a remote possibility. Even had a posse been assembled and organized, most men quickly grew tired of a long, probably pointless trek into the wilderness. Their wrath would cool quickly as the miles passed.

The bandits were now entering the narrow pass carved into the Bullhead over the eons by the flowing river, and the shadows of the monumental bluffs fell across the dusty men and weary horses. Charley Stoddard knew the area well and he led the way as they zigzagged through the gray willow trees to find the silver rill snaking its way across the sandy bottom. Higher up on the walls of the canyon, red-blooming monkey flowers grew, and atop the ridge a shaggy lone pine stood sentinel.

They swung down wearily, unsaddled their ponies and drank from the cool stream. Then, settling into the shade cast by a tangle of thorny mesquite, where red ants filed their erratic way toward their colony and swarms of gnats bothered their eyes and nostrils, they rested. Billy sat with his knees drawn up, arms looped around them. His expression was pensive, gloomy even as Pearly and Charley Stoddard counted out the money they had taken from the bank. The paper money was arranged in thick, banded blocks and errant sunbeams glittered off the shimmering stacks of gold coins.

'Cheer up, why don't you!' Pearly said to his young cousin, slapping him on the shoulder. 'You're free and rich now. Nobody's going to find our trail, no one's going to track us down. We're in the clear, Billy.'

★　★　★

'What's the bounty?' Big Jack Corrigan wanted to know. He was seated in the green-leather chair opposite Marshal Kent Pollack in the latter's office in the

Adobe Falls, New Mexico, courthouse.

Pollack lifted lazy eyes to those of the thick-chested bounty hunter. He was not fond of Corrigan, but he had his uses. No regular lawman was inclined to, nor could be expected to chase down outlaws across the thousands of square miles of southwest desert, leaving their own communities without law enforcement. Men like Jack Corrigan recognized no such boundaries, geographical or moral. A successful bounty hunter — those who did not get killed in their pursuits — could make twenty times more a year than a local marshal if he found his man. It was enough incentive for many to attempt it; only a few had the raw nerve and skills to survive. Big Jack Corrigan was one such man.

'There's a share of the stolen money, of course,' Pollack said. 'You'd have to ask the bank what they're offering.'

'I was asking about the bounty,' Jack Corrigan said in his usual bluff way. 'You never know if you're going to recover the money.' Pollack's mouth tightened; he had never liked Corrigan's manner. Maybe that was not important.

'Five hundred for Pearly Gillis,' the town marshal said. 'A dozen men recognized him.' He passed the wanted poster across his desk. 'You know Pearly?'

Corrigan nodded, tugging at his ear with broken-knuckled fingers.

'Slim Charley Stoddard is riding with him,' Pollack continued. 'Five hundred for Charley as well.'

'There were three of them.'

'Yes, well, all we know of the other man is that he's a kid, maybe still in his teens. Someone heard him called 'Billy' in a saloon a few nights ago. He just held the horses for the robbers, but that doesn't matter in the eyes of the law, as you know — he was involved in the robbery and murder as well. The bank has posted a two-hundred dollar reward for him.'

'Twelve hundred for the bunch,'

Corrigan said as he fingered his broken teeth.

'That's right.' In the days when the going pay for a ranch hand was a dollar a day, this was a considerable amount of money. The object of the game was to catch the outlaws as quickly as possible, freeing the bounty hunter for his next task. This particular bounty, however, did not promise to come easy. Pearly Gillis was no fool. He had been marauding in the territories for years; Charley Stoddard was a disgraced army scout who knew every inch of New Mexico and Arizona Territories.

Jack Corrigan rose abruptly and positioned his faded gray hat, which he had not bothered to remove for the interview. He had already made up his mind to accept the job. There was only one question left to ask as he tucked the arrest warrants into his leather vest's inner pocket.

'Dead or alive, is it then?' he asked.

Marshal Pollack nodded his affirmative. 'It was murder, Jack.'

* * *

Ken Wingate was waiting outside the marshal's office, his hat tugged low as he studied the streets of Adobe Falls. There was little to divert his attention, a hay wagon, a few barefoot kids with fishing poles racing through the town. A Mexican who looked to weigh at least 300 pounds was pushing a small cart laden with *tamales* and decorated with all sorts of shiny bangles.

The door opened beside him and Big Jack Corrigan emerged, looking satisfied. The two men walked uptown, leading their horses. Ken waited for Corrigan to start a conversation, but that wasn't the taciturn bounty hunter's way, as Wingate knew. There was a well in the center of town surrounded by lacy mesquite trees. A few women in striped skirts were drawing water there with their *ollas*. Corrigan angled that way, wanting their mounts well-watered.

'Well,' Ken Wingate said finally as the horses dipped their muzzles into the wooden trough beside the well, 'how does it figure, Jack?'

'Twelve hundred for the gang,' Big Jack told the sly little man. He wristed sweat from his forehead and leaned back against the hitching rail there.

'Not bad,' Ken said appreciatively. 'Four hundred apiece.'

'You're forgetting my son,' Corrigan said. Wingate had not forgotten the young splinter of a kid who, he had initially assumed, given time to ponder the reality of this lifestyle, would pull out. 'That makes four of us. Tabor gets his share — the same as you and Skaggs.'

'Hell, Jack,' Wingate objected, 'the kid's never even been on a bounty before. He's liable to be more trouble than he's worth! What if he can't bring up the nerve when it's time? You, me, Luke Skaggs, we know we can count on each other when the shooting starts, but the kid . . . '

'I said he's my son,' Corrigan said in that familiar stone-cold tone which meant that his mind was made up and this was the way things were going to be. 'He'll stand in a fight. It's in his blood.'

Ken Wingate was unhappy, but he tried to keep his pique out of his voice. He only nodded and answered quietly, 'Whatever you say, Jack.'

Corrigan seemed ready to grumble a response, but he swallowed his retort. The horses were showing no further interest in the water which dripped in silver beads from their muzzles, and so the two bounty hunters started on their way, still leading their horses. Although it has been fairly noted that a cowboy would rather ride his pony from one side of the street to the other than walk across it, the bounty hunters held a different philosophy. Their horses were the tools of their trade, no less than the weapons they carried. Their own ponies — the quickest and best that could be purchased — were expected to be able to run down any fleeing band of desperados whose mounts were usually more ill-used. The bounty hunters' horses were never mounted until it was time to work. Meanwhile they were kept well-rested, well-fed, well-watered, cared for as carefully as were their Colt revolvers and Winchester rifles.

A man has to maintain his edge to be successful, Big Jack Corrigan was fond of saying. His horses were a part of that edge.

The bounty hunters had earlier made their camp a little east of town where a slow-flowing creek wound its way along the sandy wash. The area was clogged with willow brush and creosote along the river bottom, but only a single, wind-ruffled sycamore stood on the flat where the other men waited.

'They're back,' Luke Skaggs said, rising from beside the low-burning fire to dust his hands on his jeans and face westward.

Tabor Corrigan, who had not heard the approaching men and horses, rose automatically, nervously. Red-headed, rail-thin and shy he wore his newly purchased handgun high on his hip, his belt tightly cinched. His hands still held the blue tin coffee cup and the half-gallon pot he had been using to fill it. Skaggs glanced at the younger man and smiled thinly. 'Don't get shaky on us, kid. Now we're going out to teach you how things are done out here.'

'I'm not shaky, Skaggs,' Tabor Corrigan shot back, trying to find an echo of his father's authoritative voice as he answered.

But he was feeling shaky. It was a feeling he could not define. He knew he was not a coward, but these bearded men he now rode with carried an aura of death about them, one and all. His mother had recently passed away down in Arkansas, and with nowhere to turn Tabor had come West after writing to his father, who had always seemed to him capable, strong, brave. As all children remember their fathers. But the man he had been reunited with — Big Jack Corrigan — was something more than that. He was a frightening

21

presence who walked in shadows and hunted by night. Tabor had come to know from the tales told around the campfire that Jack Corrigan was nothing more nor less than a hired killer.

And it scared the hell out of Tabor.

2

Sheriff Saul Archer, the law-enforcement officer putatively in charge of the vast miles of his desolate county, lifted his pouched eyes as the stranger in the doorway of his Santa Fe, New Mexico, office hesitated and waited to be invited in.

Shifting his bulk, Saul leaned toward his desk, planted his elbows on it and folded his stubby fingers together. 'You must be Saleen,' the sheriff said.

'That's right,' the tall man answered. There were still signs of travel on him, his face, though neatly shaven, was deeply sun-burned. Salt-stain whitened the front of his dark-blue shirt.

'Come in, then. Sit down and let's get to it. I need to see your papers, of course.'

Lee Saleen nodded, crossed the bare plank floor of the room and handed the sheriff his packet of authorizations. Saul Archer studied the documents slowly. It was difficult to tell if the aging lawman was dubious or simply a slow reader. Beyond the courthouse window a swarm of crows sat in the branches of a barren broken oak. The sky was crystal blue, unmarred by clouds.

Eventually the sheriff finished his perusal of the deputy United States marshal's documents and pushed the packet back across his desk. Saleen studied the man with cold blue eyes which seemed, nevertheless, to hold a twinkle of amusement. He wore no badge, and, indeed, there was none concealed about his person or in his goods. It seemed inadvisable in the wild country.

'Here's why I wrote to the US marshal's office,' Archer said in a low voice, his eyes going to the open door behind Saleen. 'We've a problem no one in the territory is equipped or willing to handle.'

'Bounty hunters,' Saleen said, crossing his legs at the knees.

'Killers is more like it. Bounty killers,' Archer said with some bitterness. He briefly stretched his stubby arms skyward. 'Don't get me wrong, Marshal Saleen, some of them — the good ones — have contributed a lot in trying to clean up the West. They can cross jurisdictions where an ordinary lawman cannot legally do so. They have unlimited time to pursue their quarry, unlike a town marshal, a county sheriff. From time to time bounty hunters have captured the worst of the worst when these outlaws would have escaped if not for their efforts.'

'But the trouble is . . . ?' Lee Saleen prompted as the sheriff lapsed into a lengthy pause.

'The trouble is, there is a small cadre of these men who think themselves above the law simply because they have legal authorization behind them. You see, Saleen, when a poster says 'dead or alive', I interpret that as meaning if there is no reasonable way of effecting a surrender and the outlaw is ready and willing to shoot it out, well . . . if it must be done, it must.

'The bounty killers, on the other hand, take it as a license to kill. No matter that they sometimes kill the wrong man first and only discover it later. There is a reason behind this behavior, as you know.' Saleen nodded; he did know. The sheriff went on: 'To cart dead men back over a hundred miles of sun-blistered desert is a most unpleasant experience. The stench, the black shadows of circling buzzards always overhead, the coyotes stalking the camp at night . . . ' Again Saul Archer lapsed into silence, perhaps recalling too vividly some experience he once had had at a similar grim task.

'As you are aware, then, Marshal Saleen, because of those difficulties, the practice evolved some years ago of gunning a man down, decapitating him and bringing his head alone in for the bounty offered. In some cases it is certain that the wrong man was killed. A few years ago we had a case of some

Indian renegades wanted for murder being shot down, their heads brought back in a gunny sack. No one had ever seen the dead men before; to them all the Indians looked the same anyway. Nevertheless the bounty hunters were paid off.'

'You suspect collusion with some local lawmen?' Saleen asked, recrossing his legs.

'Certainly,' the sheriff said with some vehemence. 'It makes the lawman look good to his community — those criminals who have been removed are no longer a threat in their district. It bolsters political ambitions and lines the officers' pockets if the bounty is divided among them, contingent on only a cursory identification and verification by the man with the badge.'

Lee Saleen removed his wide-brimmed fawn-colored hat and placed it carefully on the sheriff's scarred desk. Outside the window the crows, startled by some unseen menace, rose as one on heavy blue-black wings and swept into the sky.

'That brings us to you,' Sheriff Archer said. 'There are several of these bounty hunters whose methods we view as darkly as those of the men they pursue.' He shook his head heavily. 'It's not for me to judge whether they should be hanged as well as the outlaws, but that is the point, Saleen! All of these men, no matter how vicious, are entitled to a trial. That, Marshal, is why I have asked for you to come here.'

'I see,' Saleen said thoughtfully. How he was expected to clean up a long-festering problem that straddled ill-defined legal boundaries was beyond him, but Archer had something specific in mind.

'These are the worst of the worst,' Archer said, sliding another paper containing a list of names across to Sateen. 'We know where they are right now, we even know who they are pursuing. And, God help me! The men they are chasing deserve nothing more than a hangman's noose. But the present system cannot continue in such an unregulated manner. I want the message to get out that the methods employed by these bounty-killers is unacceptable and they will be made to pay for the way they abuse their license.

'Then,' Archer said, finally relaxing, 'maybe we can bring a new breed of bounty hunters into the game: honest men who will do honest work for an honest reward.'

'And you're counting on me to make all this happen?' Lee Saleen asked drily, and for the first time the balding sheriff smiled.

'No, sir,' Archer replied deliberately. 'I am just hoping that you can put a stop to some of this wanton killing and make a small difference, as each of us in law enforcement tries to do. An example must be made of thugs like Big Jack Corrigan and his ilk.'

*　*　*

The sheriff wasn't asking much, Lee Sateen thought as he soaked his

29

travel-weary body in a copper tub in the back room of the barber-shop. Track down four men who were out there — somewhere — pursuing a band of murderers and make them all see the error of their ways. Lee smiled grimly, rubbing his arm with the rough, pungent bar of yellow lye soap.

Of course, he wasn't paid to take on jobs that anyone else could do. He had been fortunate enough — unfortunate enough? — to have had some success tracking down some of the most elusive bandits in the West, from Texas to the Dakotas. His reputation was widely known, but as Lee knew well, a reputation did nothing to guarantee success.

He stepped from the tub and dried off with a large, rough-textured white towel. After wrapping it around his hips he stood at the small, smoky-blue window staring out at the long red desert. Several ideas had already presented themselves. Some of them he had used in the past quite successfully. Others had failed completely due to chance or poor execution. He had once managed to fall in with the very gang of outlaws he had been sent to capture. That had been a near thing, costing him a bullet wound in the calf of his right leg. Still, it had worked once and could again if everything fell into place.

Wary though Pearly Gillis and his outlaws would be, it was still a possibility, if a dim one. The second option seemed only a notch or two safer: try to join up with Big Jack Corrigan and his band of bounty hunters under some pretext. Perhaps he could convince Corrigan that he, Lee, was a disaffected member of Pearly's gang and knew their destination. Again, that was a hazardous ploy. Big Jack had been known to leave dead men behind him on his trail.

Either scenario would involve a lot of play-acting and thought. One slip-up or any whim of the killers could lead to his murder.

First of all, Lee thought as he proceeded to dress in his black jeans and a new rust-red shirt, he would have to catch up with those he pursued. Tracking alone would not work; it would always find him a day or two behind. Pearly had to be out-guessed somehow. On his mental map of the Territory, Lee sketched in the routes and towns, small pueblos that might serve as refuge, for however carefully planned Pearly's escape had been, still they must stop sometime, somewhere to rest their horses or trade them, to replenish their food supply.

To begin with, Lee knew, he would have to do some old-style Apache tracking to establish the true direction of their escape route. He hoped it was not intended to take them into Mexico because current treaties did not allow US marshals to enter the country with intention to extradite.

The bounty hunters had no such concerns. They carried no badges, relied on no warrants. As Lee positioned his hat in the broken mirror of the room, he reminded himself that before he left, he must remember to destroy the warrants he was carrying. Any careless oversight could bring instant death. He knew; he had come close on several occasions. Sighing, he wondered again at his choice of profession. Walking through the barber shop, where one man was being shaven, another reading the *Police Gazette* as he awaited his turn in the chair, Lee flipped the barber a silver dollar and went out into the fierce morning sunlight. His thoughts grew heavier as he walked to the stable where his stocky buckskin horse waited. Crossing the street through the roil of white dust left in the wake of a passing ore wagon, Lee Saleen — not for the first time in his long career — considered yet another option.

Burn the warrants, swing aboard the buckskin and ride away from his dangerous and grisly assignment. Ride out on to the clear, clean desert, across it and continue until he was far away from anyone who knew him or needed him to do their dirty work.

After all, he had a good pony and twenty-four dollars to boot.

★   ★   ★

Riding through the night had done nothing to calm Billy Gillis's feelings of imminent danger. The brutal reality was that the town of Adobe Falls might be able to mourn and then forget the memory of the murdered man in this violent land, but bank robbery would not be forgotten. Bank robbery meant that land could not be seeded, wells sunk, provisions laid up. Clothing would have to be repatched; all of men's slaving labor on a harsh desert had been blown away like dust in the wind. Lives would be ruined. Even in the inky silence of the desert night, the whispering wind sounded like the voices of pursuing men to Billy and he rode with his head constantly swiveling, watching and waiting for the angry following citizens.

Only once had he mentioned his fears to Pearly and Charley Stoddard, but both of them had laughed off his concerns.

'No sod-busters are going to track us across the desert,' Pearly had assured him.

Charley added: 'And nobody human can follow us in the dark. We've got miles on them, kid. Don't get yourself nervous over nothing.'

The words, though logical, did nothing to dispel Billy Gillis's fears. He rode on silently after that. The stars were so numerous and bright that they seemed to clot the velvet skies with a silver web. He knew he should have felt secure and safe beneath the deep blanket of night, in the company of these knowledgeable plainsmen, but he did not. He saw no one as they rode, heard nothing when they occasionally halted to rest their ponies.

But there was somebody back there. Someone on their backtrail bringing retribution and death. This knowledge and the whispered threats of the wind were too strong for Billy Gillis to ignore. He rode on, huddled in his lonely fear.

★   ★   ★

Ken Wingate had the eyes of a cat. Following the natural entrance to Bullhead Springs, he had swung down and gestured to the others to hold their horses back as he walked ahead in a half-crouch, searching the shore for fresh sign.

★   ★   ★

Starlight glinted off the face of the trickling stream and shone brightly on the silver-white quartz gravel lining the creek. The bounty hunters watched and waited as Wingate went ritualistically through his search, crouching here, there, twice lighting a match to examine some small impression in the soil.

At last he rose, stretched his narrow

arms and walked calmly back toward Big Jack Corrigan to report.

'Three horses. All shod.' Meaning that the horses were not Indian ponies.

'You sure, Ken?' Luke Skaggs asked. Wingate didn't dignify the doubting question with a response. He had been tracking outlaws off and on for fifteen years across this country and was offended when his word was questioned. Skaggs meant nothing by it. The broken-nosed, bald-headed hunter was simply unable to understand how Wingate could read all he did in the tangle of tracks and natural depressions.

'Where will they be heading, then?' Big Jack Corrigan asked, stroking his fingers through his gray-streaked black beard.

'Not Mexico,' Ken Wingate replied, shaking his head. 'They've watered their ponies, but from here on there's nothing to the south. A man had better damn well plan his route in this country, Jack.' He looked up at the starry skies, at the bulky mesas looming above them. 'Their next stop will have to be Camden Creek. There's no water anyplace else nearby that I know of. Maybe the Indians know of a few *tinajas*, but even Charley Stoddard, all the time he's spent on the desert, is unlikely to know of them. Besides, those are hidden waterholes and this bunch — like all crooks — will want to beeline out of the territory, not fool around playing hide-and-seek.'

'You're saying Arizona Territory?' Jack Corrigan asked. Ken Wingate nodded again.

'I'd bet on it, Jack. We have to remember that they do have Charley Stoddard riding with them, though, and he's got a bag of tricks if he starts to get suspicious about someone following them.'

'Water your ponies, boys,' Jack Corrigan instructed them now that Wingate had completed his search and drawn his conclusions. 'We'll camp here.'

'We've got to take the time to get to high ground come morning, Jack,' Wingate told their leader as the horses drank from the night-silvered waters of the Bullhead. 'It'll be slower, but you can bet that they'll be riding the rimrock so they can see their backtrail. Charley Stoddard will see to that.'

'Yes, you're right,' Big Jack said. He was crouched on his heels, watching his horse drink, watching the faint dim glow of the late-rising moon. 'I just hope you're right about Arizona being their destination.'

'Jack . . .' Wingate said with a hint of indignation.

'Yes, yes, I know,' Jack Corrigan said holding up a placating hand. 'You're only right ninety-five per cent of the time.' He attempted a smile, an expression so unpracticed that it was always unconvincing. He rose heavily from his crouch and stretched his back.

'I believe you're right, Ken. Know you are. Even if somehow your guess is wrong, it doesn't really matter. Because sooner or later, I will track down Pearly Gillis and his gang. Sooner or later all of them are going to meet the devil.'

3

Lee Saleen tugged his hat low, squinting into the rising sun which was only now cresting the eastern hills. His buckskin horse flushed a coyote with a black-tailed jackrabbit in its jaws, and it slunk away at their approach. High in the pale sky a red-tailed hawk was circling, seeking its own, smaller prey. On the desert everything was hunter or quarry. Lizards, snakes, rabbits and puma alike. Lee followed his own prey doggedly by the early light.

Following the bounty hunters had become effortless at this point. They were strung out in a direct line toward Arizona Territory. When he first cut their sign they had been riding cautiously, slowly sweeping back and forth, casting about for their own quarry. Now, it seemed, someone among them had found their spoor and guessed the destination of the

Pearly Gillis gang. It was not surprising, even considering the vastness surrounding them. The bounty hunters made their living following these rough trails and they knew them well.

Lee Saleen let his buckskin stretch out into a longer stride in the still-cool morning, closing the gap between himself and the hunters. His horse was strong and a good runner, but still it was a futile way to go about matters. What he needed to do was to get ahead of the killers and their pursuers, and this was not as impossible as it seemed.

Not so many miles to the south the new railroad, the Arizona & Eastern line, had recently been completed. If he could somehow meet one of their trains along the way, he could cut miles and hours, if not days, from his search. He reined in his horse, cuffed the sweat from his eyes and considered as he looked out across the white desert where the sun, growing strength and altitude now stunned his vision.

He could be wrong, of course. But he

knew that the railroad terminus was Yuma. There was no way the bank robbers could ride that far without fresh horses, not in summertime conditions. Tucson, Lee believed, was on the line also. It, too was hundreds of miles distant. But Fort Thomas was not so far away, situated along the Lower Gila River. If Lee was correct, the railroad with its military contract would certainly pass quite near to the army outpost. Else what use was it to settlers and army forces?

Lee started his horse on again as the sun rose higher and a blast-furnace wind began to blow off the mountains. He rode on more slowly out of deference to his buckskin and because he knew that now that he had committed to a plan of action, haste made no difference. He would either be able to catch a ride on a westbound train or find himself impossibly far behind the riders ahead.

For now, as he walked his pony steadily south-westerly, he had to assume — to convince himself — that his instincts were correct. It would be at Tucson, or nearby, where the Gillis gang would surface. He would only have to wait and remain ready. Someone would talk. Someone would brag. Men do not rob banks to hide their money away in a hole in the ground. Not after riding days across the blistering desert.

Pearly Gillis, or one of his band, would be thirsty for whiskey, hungry for women and the frustrations of the long road would lead them into some settlement searching for whatever civilized comforts they could find.

There were the horses to be considered as well, of course. Even if the gang knew of sources of water — Lee did not know of many — the days of rugged travel were bound to take their toll on their mounts. There was only the poorest possible forage out on the desert, and they would have to keep moving, always moving.

Not that they would have any great

fear of being tracked down. They would know that Marshal Pollack from Adobe Falls would not chase them this far. They could not know about the bounty hunters. And so the bank robbers would be cautious, but no longer greatly in fear of being caught. They would begin to relax after another day or so. Not completely but, Lee thought, just enough to lose their edge.

Lee could now make out the distant shapes of the buildings at Fort Thomas. Far distant, they appeared as matchboxes grouped across the sandy flatlands. He rode on, a little grimly, knowing that if all his suppositions were accurate, there was still the one formidable snag in his plan.

He was a lone rider on the desert, pursuing seven armed and dangerous men.

★   ★   ★

The morning sun above the notched hills was a magnet drawing all the colors of the sky to it, flaring red and then deep orange. It was surprisingly cool in the shallow arroyo where Ken Wingate was once again crouched down to study the tracks the bank robbers had left behind. Young Tabor Corrigan watched with fascination as the patient old tracker drew his conclusions.

Tabor wished he had not joined his father and these rough, bearded men. Whatever romantic idea he might have had about tracking down criminals had been swept away by the endless ride, the blistering desert wind, the thirst and poker-hot sun on his back.

Wingate rose, wiping his hands together and managed a nearly tooth-less smile. 'These are their tracks, all right. I can read them from a pony's back by now. The horses are beat up pretty good, Jack. Just like we thought.'

'I told you that when we found no night camp.'

'We made night camp,' young Tabor ventured. The others glanced at him, amused by his ignorance.

Jack Corrigan explained to his son: 'There's a difference between them and us, Tabor. We camped to rest ourselves and our mounts. Tracking at night is doubtful business. Pearly, on the other hand, is trying to make all the miles he can under cover of darkness. The thing is — night riding is a hazardous enterprise. You lose your landmarks. Your horse steps in a rabbit hole it didn't see. You stray off into some brushy arroyo by mistake and spend half of your time trying to work your way back out of it.'

'Come mornin',' Luke Skaggs chipped in after spitting out a stream of tobacco juice, some of which dribbled into his streaked beard, 'they're riding weary horses, and they're angry and tired themselves, having taken no rest. Oh, our way is best,' he finished, spitting once again.

'We can cover twice the ground they can this morning,' Jack Corrigan told his son. 'Now we've got light of day and fresh ponies under us.'

'Why then does Pearly Gillis push it so . . . ?'

'Pearly Gillis has to be wary of men on his trail,' Jack said. 'Us, we've no such trouble. Patience, son, is a hunting man's friend.'

As they moved on, the sand began to change to silver again. The low hills that crowded around them took on form and contour as they emerged from the night shadows. Within an hour of daybreak the desert sun was as hot on Tabor's back as ever it had been.

'I don't much like Pearly riding at night myself,' Luke Skaggs commented as they rode up out of the wash and continued across the flats, their horses walking steadily. 'Do you think we've spooked him, Ken? I mean, mayhap they reached high ground sooner than we thought and took a long look down their backtrail, saw us.'

Ken Wingate was thoughtful. 'Could be,' he agreed. 'But I don't think so. I think he's just getting antsy. This morning, what are they doing again?

Beelining it south-west. No, Pearly doesn't know we're back here yet. By the time he figures it out it'll be too late.'

Then what was going to happen? Tabor tried not to think about it. At twenty he had been only in a few fist-fights of the schoolyard variety and had never drawn a gun on a man — especially not a hardened criminal. Big Jack, Wingate and Luke Skaggs seemed completely unconcerned about shooting it out or being shot.

Worse, last night in their tiny camp the three older men had been swapping stories again as they prepared to roll up in their blankets. Tabor had remained curled up in his bed. They reminded Tabor of a gang of pirates with their dark amusement at the fate of some of their captured men. He wished he could just ride away, but he could not. Where would he go, not knowing this land? How could he survive on his own? Lingering among his fears was also the wish to prove himself a man to his father, to be like Jack Corrigan. Big, gruff and respected in the raw land. He could not show himself up as a coward.

Now he rode on with silent remorse beneath the molten sun. He heard Big Jack say, 'Let's put some miles behind us, boys,' as he lifted his blue roan into a ground-devouring canter. The others followed suit and soon they were racing across the flatlands in pursuit of their foe, the unwilling Tabor Corrigan following them stride for stride, angry with himself, with his father and quite unwilling to embrace the bloodshed and death to come.

★ ★ ★

Pearly Gillis stood in his stirrups, cursing violently as the furnace wind of the long desert raked his body, pawed mockingly at his shirt, and twisted his Appaloosa's mane and tail. Charley Stoddard sat silently beside Pearly, his eyes studying the rocky arroyo below. The fringes on his buckskin shirt danced in the wind like hundreds of tiny whips.

'Well, damn all, Charley! Where's the water? This can't be Camden Creek.'

'I'm afraid it is, Pearly,' Charley replied, mopping at his forehead with his red scarf. 'I've seen it like this before after a dry winter in the mountains. When there's good run-off it'll flow six feet deep and twenty across.'

'That's not doing us a damned bit of good now, is it, Charley!' Pearly snapped, as if the lack of rainfall in the uplands was somehow Charley Stoddard's fault.

Billy Gillis sat, sun-stunned, staring out across the empty land.

'We'd best find a place to hole up until after dark,' Charley said. 'When it cools, we can push on a little further.'

'Toward where, Charley!' Pearly said with even more ferocity. 'We don't get some water soon, our horses are going to drop. Then we can walk on until *we* drop.' He glanced skyward at a lone ominous buzzard circling in the white sky like an early omen.

'Give the ponies what's left in our canteens,' Charley said, shrugging one thin shoulder. 'After sundown we walk them on. Maybe we'll spot a light from some pueblo or small ranch.'

'And maybe we won't!' Pearly spat. Billy had never seen his cousin quite like this. There was a killing anger in his deep-set eyes and his Apache features were fixed, his mouth only a thin bitter line. This, then, was the Pearly Gillis men feared. It was when he was frustrated in not being able to get what he needed when he wanted it that Pearly became more than dangerous. He walked the thin line between his rage and madness. Billy had to look away, and as he did he saw the small approaching figures far out on the desert flats, riding slowly toward them through rising veils of heat.

'Pearly?' Billy managed to say through parched lips. 'Someone's coming.'

Pearly's eyes switched to the south-west where the three horsemen appeared and disappeared behind the rippling heat veils like ghost riders. He squinted into the distance, his eyes expressionless now. His anger seemed to have waned, his mind to become more once coolly calculating.

'What do you want to do, Pearly?' Charley Stoddard asked. 'We can dip into the wash and belly up to the rim with our Winchesters.'

'No. We don't even know who they are. Why make them suspicious?' He paused and then said decisively, 'But you, Charley, take one of these little feeders and lose yourself.'

'All right,' Charley said without question. He had turned his gray horse away from the others when Pearly added without glancing at him:

'Make sure you know your landmark.'

Charley nodded and rode on, descending a sandy wash which funneled into the rocky arroyo. Billy Gillis, his mouth drier than ever, his hands trembling as he clenched the pommel of his saddle, asked:

'Is Charley going to cover us?'

'If it comes to that he will,' Pearly said, his eyes fixed on the incoming riders. 'Mainly he's going to stash the loot from the bank where nobody but us can ever find it again. That's what this is all about, after all, Billy. The money.'

The desert wind gusted and shifted the white sands. Billy's mouth had been dry before. Now his tongue cleaved to his palate. His eyes burned. As the three approaching riders neared the arroyo, Billy now could see that they carried their rifles across their saddle-bows. Sunlight glinted on metal. One man wore a silver hatband on his Stetson. It gleamed in the white sunlight like a shimmering halo. Billy glanced at Pearly, but his cousin showed no concern. His deep-set eyes, shadowed by the brim of his hat, were unreadable. Was this where Billy was going to have to fight and die — out here in this stone and sand wilderness where a jackrabbit would have trouble surviving, where his bleached bones would never be discovered?

'Pearly — '

'Shut up.' The riders neared the opposite bank of the wide, stony arroyo. They slowed their horses, exchanged unheard words and started forward again at a walk. The horsemen opposite drew up and halted. Their leader, the one with the silver hatband, tilted his black hat back and called out.

'Hello, Pearly! Thought I recognized that Appaloosa pony of yours. Where's Charley Stoddard?'

'Flanked out, Cody. We couldn't tell who was riding in.'

'No sense waiting there for the river to run!' The man Pearly had called Cody laughed. 'Come on across. I've got a little hideout not far from here. We've got water.'

Pearly's expression now briefly showed doubt. But they had no choice. They were not going to ride further on their thirsty, weary mounts.

'Who is he?' Billy asked in a taut whisper.

'Man I met in my travels. Cody Minor's his name,' Pearly answered in an equally low tone.

'Do you trust him?'

'I trust no man.' Then, lifting his voice so it could be heard across the rocky arroyo, Pearly called, 'Thanks for the invite, Cody. We'd be much obliged.'

With a nod to Billy, Pearly turned his leggy appaloosa horse toward the feeder wash where Charley Stoddard had earlier disappeared. As he reached the fork in the arroyo, Charley appeared, his rifle at the ready.

'Is that who I think it is?' Charley asked.

'Yes. These old ghosts just continue to pop up. You get the job done?' Pearly asked as they rode up the wash, looking for an easy way up the other side. Charley, with a quick glance at Billy Gillis, nodded his answer. Finding a sandy ramp the horses could climb easily, they rode up on to the flats to find that Cody Minor and his two men had been waiting for them. The strangers had sheathed their rifles, and Cody was all smiles as he shook hands with Pearly and Charley Stoddard. He looked questioningly at Billy.

'My cousin, Billy,' Pearly said, and Cody extended his hand again. He wore a white shirt and black jeans, that black hat with the silver band and a low-riding ivory-handled .44 revolver. His two companions looked too alike to be anything but brothers. Youngish men with vacant blue eyes and tightly curled, coppery hair.

'This is Warren Spangler, his brother Virgil,' Cody said. Neither man offered his hand. 'My place is about an hour on, Pearly. It's as dry as anywhere else, but we keep a freight wagon fitted with eight one-hundred gallon barrels. Every couple of weeks we haul water up from Tucson.'

'You ride into that town?' Pearly asked as they started on toward the head of a small canyon where the Camden had its source in wetter times.

Cody laughed. 'Not me, Pearly! They've got the railroad now, and where the railroad goes, the telegraph follows. I send a man.'

They entered the canyon where shadows from the high-rising chocolate bluffs cast the welcome relief of shade. They rode silently for most of the way after that, Cody leading the way, Pearly beside him. Charley Stoddard and Billy followed next with the vacant-looking Spangler brothers trailing.

The trail made two elbow turns — one right, one left, then they emerged on to a dry valley surrounded by jumbled hills. They passed acre-sized stands of nopal cactus, low useless clumps of dry yellow grass, greasewood and scattered yucca. There was one large willow tree so dry and barren that it looked as if it had been burned over. Eventually they passed through a stand of huge yellow boulders — a perfect site for watching men, and came upon the hideout.

There was a low stone building

showing a blunt, windowless face and, further to the north, toward the encroaching, broken hills, there were two smaller stone buildings, a lean-to where horses were sheltered and a small tool shed. Next to this stood a freight wagon with six-foot high wheels. There were four water barrels strapped to each side of this.

Billy thought that he should have been feeling some relief now. These men had water, some shade and comfort to offer and the sun was already beginning to descend. Soon it would be cooler, soon he would have quenched his thirst, maybe have found a bed for the first time in days.

Why then did he feel that he had only been snatched from the promise of a blistering death on the desert wasteland to be delivered here to die?

★ ★ ★

'What do you make of it, Ken?' Big Jack Corrigan asked the lanky trailsman. He

59

himself had swung down from his blue roan's back to give it some relief. Slapping his trail-dusty pants with his wide gray hat he waited until Ken was sure enough to make his observations known.

'Their horses were struggling. You can see that by their shortened gait and occasional halt step. They were gambling all on the Camden Creek water. No one could have known it was dried up. I wouldn't have guessed it.'

'Go on,' Jack Corrigan said impatiently. All of that he had already known. He was dry, sun-weary and short-tempered himself.

'I tracked them down into the arroyo,' Ken said, wiping his narrow face with his scarf, 'and up the far side.'

Jack Corrigan's face again showed uncharacteristic impatience. Hadn't he known all *that* as well? He was the one who had sent Ken looking while the rest of them rested their ponies.

'Well!'

'They met up with the others on the

opposite bank and — '

'*What* others!'

'I don't know, Jack. Pearly and his gang joined up with three men riding in from the south.' Ken Wingate tied his scarf around his neck again. Ken lifted a bony finger toward the canyon mouth to the west. 'All of 'em, in a group, headed up into the hills.'

'What's up there?' Big Jack demanded.

'No idea, Jack. Nothin' I've ever seen or heard of. Could be some kind of robbers' roost, I suppose.'

No one spoke for a long minute. Tabor Corrigan stood holding his weary sorrel by its bridle, stroking its salt-flecked muzzle. Luke Skaggs was looking in his saddle-bags with growing disappointment for another twist of chewing tobacco. Big Jack had replaced his faded gray hat, and he stood, his shirt pasted to his chest with perspiration, watching the foothills like a frustrated general plotting his next assault.

'All right,' he said at last. 'We wait.'

'We . . . wait?' Tabor Corrigan said, staring blankly at his father. The bearded man nodded, not returning his son's gaze.

'We wait, men. Pearly and his gang went up that canyon. I don't care why. I don't care who he went with. He went up there and they will come out again. When they do,' Big Jack Corrigan promised, 'we will be waiting, and we will cut them down one by one.'

4

In the smoky interior of Cody Minor's house the men sat around the long plank table, drinking whiskey and coffee. Billy Gillis withdrew as far as possible from the group, seating himself on a chair made from a barrel in the far corner. There were Indian rugs hung on the walls for decorations, a heavy-beamed ceiling and a massive stone fireplace. In the corner lay the dying man on his poor cot.

Sweat glistened on his broad fore-head. His eyes stared at the ceiling almost unblinkingly. He seemed untended; his fate had only been discussed once in a light manner as they had first entered the house.

'Is that old Woody Skyler?' Pearly Gillis had asked.

'Yeah. Fell and broke his leg, did old Woodrow,' Cody had replied.

'Looks more like lead poisoning to me,' Charley Stoddard said drily. After that no one mentioned the dying man again.

The interior of the house was smoky, suffocating even with the door standing open. Cody Minor had set out two bottles of bourbon and yelled to his fat Mexican cook to boil coffee. Then he had retreated to the interior of the house, appearing in a fresh pair of dark trousers, a clean white shirt with a black-string tie, his hair slicked back.

After a single cup of coffee Billy had seated himself alone. Now, as time passed and the older men continued to drink and tell tales of their backtrails, he rose and walked out on to the porch, feeling eyes on his back.

'Where you going, Billy?' Pearly asked.

'Want to see to my horse. Need some air.'

'The horses are in good hands,' Cody Minor said. The Spangler brothers had insisted on watering the ponies and stabling them up.

'Still need some air,' Billy said, stepping across the threshold into the settling dusk. The sky was a dull red, the land deep violet. Only the peaks of the broken hills were still lighted by the sun. Their craggy summits held bright golden reminders of the day. Billy crossed the yard slowly, noticing a ring of whitewashed stones where someone once, long ago, had planted something — flowers? — which had long withered away.

With no other place to go, Billy did start out toward the lean-to affair where their horses had been taken. He was within a few yards of the lean-to when he heard voices and bootsteps approaching. A wariness that was becoming habitual caused him to pause and slip behind the tool-shed. The Spangler brothers passed by within feet of him.

'Looks like Cody was right,' the bigger, younger man, Virgil, said.

'He usually is,' his brother replied.

'A man like Charley Stoddard doesn't ride the wild country without even a pair of saddle-bags.'

'They've got something stashed somewhere,' Warren Spangler agreed. The voices faded away. Night settled. Billy Gillis felt a chill beyond the slowly spreading coolness. Should he report what he had heard to Pearly? Pearly, he decided, probably already knew what Cody was up to. Each man was at work, trying to outsmart the other. Pearly was winning the small battle to this point. They had watered their horses, found food and lodging. Cody was still fishing. But he would be watching, that was certain. How could Cody Minor know that Pearly was riding with a small fortune?

The telegraph, Billy realized. He remembered them talking about it on the trail. Billy removed his hat, wiped his forehead and ran his fingers through his dark curly hair. He no longer felt merely fearful. He felt doomed. He cursed himself for being foolish enough ever to have taken the outlaw trail.

66

Slowly, through the settling twilight, he started back toward the house without having visited his dun pony. He heard movement in the darkness and halted again. It took him a minute to locate the source of the sound. Then he saw the shadowy figure standing in the bed of the huge freight wagon, using a stick to measure the amount of water left in the barrels strapped to its sides.

The stranger's head came up as Billy crossed the gravel yard, and a voice called out in a fierce, half-whisper from the freight wagon's bed.

'Who are you!' The voice had an odd quality Billy couldn't immediately define.

'Who are *you?*' he responded, his hand drifting near the butt of his holstered Colt.

'I live here. I ask the questions.' Then she — it was a girl — tossed aside her measuring stick and clambered down from the high wagon to face him in the darkness, her hands on her hips, her hatless dark hair catching a raven-wing sheen from the lingering light. 'I'll ask you again,' she said, cocking her head at him.

'My name's Billy. Billy Gillis. I rode in with the others.'

'Gillis?' the girl asked. She was nearly a foot shorter than Billy and she had to look up at his face as she approached. 'Not related to that killer Pearly Gillis?'

Billy almost blurted out a defense of Pearly, but did not. 'I'm his cousin,' he admitted.

'A little young to be riding with that mob, aren't you?'

'I suppose so,' Billy said weakly. He was starting to think he was. Instead of answering directly, he said, 'You didn't tell me who you were.'

'Vida,' the girl said, her eyes never wavering. 'Vida Minor — and don't ask me if I'm related to Cody, because I am. I'm his sister. What's the gathering all about?' she asked, waving a hand toward the house. 'They figuring out a way to kill some more people?'

'I don't think — '

'Never mind,' Vida said. 'I don't want to know. I never want to know, I just do. It's hard not to when you live with a bunch of thugs and killers.'

She turned sharply away from Billy and started back toward the house. He followed a few steps behind, wondering about her. At the porch he hesitated as Vida stepped up and entered the house. By firelight her young face was more than pretty. Her dark hair shone, catching fiery highlights. He heard her say:

'We've only got about fifty gallons of water left, Cody. If you don't want us to all shrivel up and blow away, we've got to make a run into Tucson.'

'All right,' Billy heard Cody's silky voice answer.

'Well!' Vida said impatiently. 'Who's going along? Woody usually takes me in.' She looked at the dying man. 'It's pretty obvious he's not up to it.'

'I'll go,' Virgil Spangler said. The big kid's eyes were sweeping hungrily over Vida's body.

'I need you here,' Cody said after a moment's thought. It was then that Billy stepped through the doorway, removing his hat. He paused as he crossed the threshold and watched Cody's eyes shift to him. 'The kid will drive you down. You don't mind, do you, Pearly?'

'No,' Pearly Gillis said calculatingly. He knew full well that Cody wanted to make sure he had the advantage in the number of guns. It would be three against two if trouble started. Pearly gave none of that away. 'The kid's the only one without a poster out on him. It make sense.'

'Is that all right with you, Vida?' Cody asked.

'What do I care,' she answered sharply. 'I just want some water.'

With that she walked away into the inner recesses of the ranch house. Billy watched her, wondering still. There was a secret feeling of relief flooding through him. When the two gangs started squabbling over the stolen gold, he would be out of gunshot range. Perhaps, he thought distantly, when the inevitable happened, he would find himself far away from all of them. He had already had enough of the owl-hoot trail.

★ ★ ★

'Now what?' Big Jack Corrigan wondered out loud as the purple silence of dawn was rattled by the creak of heavy wagon hubs, the shriek of a brake, the plodding clop of a two-horse team. As he scrambled out of his blankets, stiff from a night spent sleeping on the rocky desert floor, he jacked a cartridge into the chamber of his Winchester and signaled to the others to stay low.

Within minutes they were able to make out the hulking figure of a freight wagon easing its way out of the canyon mouth on to the flats.

'Is that them?' Luke Skaggs whispered.

'Can't tell, wait a minute,' Big Jack answered.

'Has to be,' Luke said.

'Can't be,' the sharp-eyed Ken Wingate responded. 'It's been a while since I seen one, but unless I'm going blind, one of them's a girl.'

'Damned if he's not right,' Skaggs whispered. Tabor Corrigan was beside his father, his hands tightly squeezing the rifle in his hands, hoping — praying — that this was not the killing time.

'The other one's a kid,' Ken Wingate said. 'Could be this 'Billy' that's supposed to be riding with Pearly.'

'Could be not,' Jack Corrigan said, brushing away the gnats from his eyes. 'Could be there's some small ranches up that canyon. Could be they got nothing to do with Pearly Gillis.'

'So what do we do?' Luke Skaggs asked as the wagon across the arroyo slowly passed and turned toward the south, toward Tucson.

Big Jack was sitting, Indian-fashion on the stony earth now, still considering matters. 'They're going for water, that much is for sure,' he said after a lengthy pause. 'Whether for Pearly or not, there's no telling. We need water as well. Need it bad, but we can't chance leaving our position in case Pearly does show himself.'

'Then what do we do?' Skaggs asked.

'That wagon will be hauling water back. If it's for Pearly, he'll feel the loss if it doesn't reach him. If it's for some small rancher or other, tough. We need the water ourselves. Skaggs,' Big Jack said, making up his mind, 'trail them into Tucson, if that's where they're heading, and it seems it must be. Let them fill those water barrels. On the way back, bide your time, and then get that wagon.'

'They might not agree to that, Jack,' Skaggs said doubtfully.

'It's only a kid and a girl, Skaggs,' Jack Corrigan said in a voice that chilled young Tabor Corrigan's bones. 'Get after them.'

★ ★ ★

Vida Minor was a pretty little thing, Billy Gillis couldn't help but notice as he continued to steal glances at her from the seat of the freight wagon, but her manner was as dry as the desert wind. She wore a man's old flop hat with a yellow scarf tied around it, a blue shirt too large for her and loose twill trousers. She held her small hands clasped between her knees. Her hazel eyes, flecked with gold, remained fixed on the horizon. She had rebuffed every attempt at conversation; Billy could not tell if she had disliked him on sight or if this was simply her regular demeanor.

Two hours on as the distant, scattered buildings of Tucson came into view, Billy tried again. 'Almost there.'

She nodded at the obvious observation, but did not look his way. In growing frustration, Billy asked more emotionally, 'Have I done something to make you dislike me, Vida?'

'I don't like any of you,' she said with the briefest of glances.

'Who do you mean?' he asked,

genuinely puzzled.

'All of you men with your guns strapped down and your eyes open for the main chance,' Vida said with sudden heat.

'I'm not . . . ' he began, and then realized that he *was* one of them. At least in Vida's eyes. 'Why don't *you* pull out?' he asked her.

'Why don't you?'

'Me?' He hesitated, 'I guess because I don't have anyplace else to go.'

'You've answered your own question,' she said, and she jerked the pole whip from its socket and popped it over the ears of the plodding horses.

'You like Tucson?' Billy asked for something to say.

'Not particularly. But it's a place to see normal people going about ordinary day-to-day business, not figuring out who they're going to rob or harm next . . . when someone is going to find them and shoot them down.'

They drove on in silence. Billy could think of nothing else to say. It hurt him to know that she lumped him in with the rest of the robbers, but what could he say? He was among them and there was no way out now.

★   ★   ★

Lee Saleen sat on a wooden chair in the narrow ribbon of shade the hotel awning cast over the boardwalk. He was wondering if he had outsmarted himself in hopping that Tucson freight train out of Fort Thomas. He had been certain in his own mind that the fleeing outlaws, the bounty hunters or both would sooner or later have to make Tucson for supplies, rest . . . and water! Always water in this country. Therefore he had taken up residence in the white-frame two-story hotel on Main Street. By day he could be found sitting in that wooden chair, watching those arriving, those departing. By nights he roamed the dozen or so saloons nearby, listening to casual conversations, watching the groups of men who tramped in and out.

He had never seen any of the men he hunted, but he had committed to memory the descriptions that Sheriff Archer had written down for him. He had seen a number of men who came close to the descriptions, but observation and discreet inquiries had eliminated them from his list of suspicion.

Well, so then, Saleen thought, stretching his long arms overhead as he yawned, perhaps he had guessed wrong. It would certainly not be the first time he had erred. Tracking a man, or men, out in this wild country was always a project fraught with the chance of failure.

The morning warmth was growing uncomfortable. Lee was considering retreating to the small café in the hotel's interior when he heard the rumbling of a huge freight wagon approaching. There was nothing unusual about such a wagon — they rolled through the streets all day, bringing supplies, hauling ore from the local mines, coal to the railroad depot. But this one was different somehow. Lee tugged his hat lower and squinted into the glare of day, studying the passing wagon.

It carried no freight. It was designed for another purpose. Eight large water barrels were strapped to its sides. Perhaps it was owned by some local rancher working his spread in dry country. The driver was a young man with dark curly hair. Beside him rode a young girl, her face set and unhappy. They could be brother and sister, Lee thought, or a young married couple trying to make a living in a harsh land. Somehow he didn't think so.

He rose lazily from his chair and followed the wagon toward the east end of town where the wells were located. He stopped a passing miner and asked him, 'Do you recognize those people?'

Peering into the sun, the old man said in a lowered voice. 'I do. The girl. Why do you want to know?'

'Simple curiosity.'

'Don't get too curious, friend. The girl is Cody Minor's sister, Vida.'

'Cody Minor?' Lee said. 'Who's he?'

78

'If you don't know,' the miner said, 'you don't need to know.' With that the man stepped around Lee and continued on his way up the boardwalk.

More curious than ever, Lee continued on his way, finding the wagon drawn up beside twin wells on a plaza surrounded by low adobe buildings and scattered lacy mesquite trees. The barrels were being filled rapidly by many hands. Half a dozen Mexican men in straw sombreros passed buckets up into the bed of the wagon to be poured into the barrels. Along with these were three or four men who seemed to be local whiskey-tramps willing to work for nickels to buy their morning pick-me-ups. There were also a couple of lean young cowboys who, judging by their banter and attitudes, were willing to work for the chance of meeting a pretty young girl. Which she was, Lee could see now that she had taken off that battered flop hat and shared an occasional bright smile with the workers. Those eight one-hundred gallon barrels would be filled in no time at all.

Lee had considered going to the local law to find out something about this Cody Minor, but it seemed he had little time to spare. Following yet another hunch he walked instead back toward the stable where his buckskin horse was sheltered. No logical deduction led him, but judging from what he had heard, Cody Minor was one bad citizen. And, Lee knew, bad dogs tend to run together.

Besides, that wooden chair was getting no softer as the days went by.

★   ★   ★

Perspiration dripped into Luke Skagg's dark eyes, stinging them. The devil wind had begun to rise again, blowing drift sand from place to place. There was a long reddish upcropping of volcanic stone shaped like a broken, blunted cockscomb, some fifty feet high and hundreds of yards in length beside him. There Luke sat and waited, in the feeble shade of a trio of tall flowering ocotillo bushes, cursing his luck. This bounty was not going as any of them had envisioned it. By rights, Skaggs thought, this job should have gone to the kid. So what if he was Big Jack's son? He was going to have to prove himself sooner or later.

Skaggs tried to spit out a stream of tobacco juice. His mouth was so dry that he barely managed it. He took the smallest sip of water from his canteen and recorked it. He removed his hat, dabbed at his bald head and cursed the day, the desert and Big Jack. If there were another way to make as much money as he did on a bounty hunt, he would pull out in a moment. If . . .

Luke Skaggs's head came up, and he rose to his feet, dusting his hands on his pants. Distantly he had heard a small squeal, a rattle. Peering across the flats, he made out the slowly approaching water wagon nearing his position.

At last! Skaggs had no concerns now

that the time for action was here. He knew his work. The kid and the little girl would prove no obstacle. Grab the wagon, deliver it to Big Jack, then tell Jack frankly that if he was going to be given this kind of dog work instead of the kid, he wanted a bigger share. He walked through the deep sand to where his horse waited in the scant shade of the ocotillos.

★   ★   ★

Billy Gillis guided the lumbering wagon eastward in silence. He had tried to start up a conversation with Vida Minor, but she was even less open to it than she had been on the way into Tucson. The miles passed with only the squeaking of the wagon hubs, the slow thumping plod of the horses' hoofs. The wind rose and fell, occasionally emitting small gusting noises. Otherwise the world was only a sandy, heated silence. Vida unexpectedly touched his arm.

'There's a rider coming toward us,'

she said, peering toward the west.

'I can't see anyone.'

'He's there. From time to time you can see him behind that red upcropping.'

'One of us?' Billy asked, though why anyone from the hideout would come out to meet them was beyond him.

Vida shook her head. 'Anyone from the ranch would hail us and come ahead.'

'Just a passing rider, heading for Tucson,' Billy said more matter-of-factly than he felt. He, too, now kept his eyes on the low red ridge, once believing — or imagining — that he also saw a rider lurking there.

After another half-mile, Vida said, 'We'll find out now. He's coming this way.'

The incoming rider was no one Billy Gillis had ever seen before. A glance at Vida told him that she didn't know the man either. Stocky, bearded, the man had a broken nose that did nothing to enhance the appearance of his moon-shaped face. Billy handed Vida the reins.

'Here, take the team,' he said, lowering his right hand to rest near the butt of his holstered revolver. It was probably nothing, he thought. A man wanting directions to Tucson, wanting to ask for some water. But the man had a dangerous aspect. How he wished Pearly was here now.

The rider held up a hand, and after a minute's hesitation, Vida reined in the team. The rider circled his horse to Billy's side of the wagon. He was smiling, but the yellow-toothed expression was not reassuring. *Draw your pistol*, Billy encouraged himself, but he could not do it. By the time he might have actually done it, it was too late. The strange rider had his Winchester out and pointed at Billy's chest.

'Get down, the two of you,' he said in a voice far from friendly.

'What are you going to do?' Vida asked with surprising fierceness.

'Get mad if you don't do what I tell you!'

Belatedly, Billy decided to try it. His

84

hand twitched toward his pistol grips, but the man had been waiting for such a movement. He slammed the barrel of his rifle against Billy's wrist, numbing his hand. Then he leaned out of the saddle, grabbed Bill's shirt and yanked him from the bench seat to tumble roughly to the desert floor.

'If you only knew who I am . . . ' Vida spat.

'I only know who you'll be if you don't do as I say,' Luke Skaggs said. 'One dead little girl. Get down from that wagon, honey.'

Skaggs backed his horse a little, glancing down at Billy who was not going to give him any more trouble. Blood trickled from his nose. He was breathing roughly, his body curled against the white sand.

Skaggs smiled with grim triumph. Situation well under control. He wondered, should he take his time with the woman, shoot the kid if he interfered? He deserved some sort of reward for spending the morning sitting in the sun and wind-drifted sand.

Vida, her face furious, slipped down the far side of the wagon. Skaggs grinned and started toward her. The crack of a rifle sounded from the ridge behind him and he felt the searing impact of a bullet boring through his upper arm. The rifle fell from his paralyzed fingers as he twisted in the saddle to see the faceless man on a stubby buckskin horse riding slowly toward them.

Skaggs panicked and slapped the spurs to his pony. Riding with one hand on the reins, he contorted unnaturally to draw his pistol as his horse broke into a dead run across the sand flats. A second rifle shot was fired in his direction, this one missing wide. Skaggs threw an equally wide pistol shot across his shoulder, hoping to slow his pursuer.

It did no good. Skaggs felt his hat blow off; his pony misstepped but continued to run. Skaggs dipped into a shallow gully, racing onward. If he could reach Big Jack in time, his ambusher was in for a hell of a surprise.

His pony had trouble scrambling up the rocky slope opposite, skidded back and then rolled. Skaggs was thrown to the ground to slide to the bottom of the arroyo. He lurched to his feet and was limping away when the rider appeared above him, silhouetted against the pale desert sky.

'You son of a bitch!' Luke Skaggs screamed, firing his pistol twice. His snarl was answered by a single rifle shot that tagged him high on the chest and sent him sprawling, his pistol dropping free of his nerveless fingers.

Luke Skaggs did not live to shout another oath. He lay motionless, lifeless against the uncaring desert floor.

Lee Saleen sheathed his rifle and started back toward the freight wagon.

5

Vida Monor was crouched down beside Billy Gillis, holding his head up, rinsing his bloody face with a damp cloth. She looked up at Lee Saleen as he walked his buckskin horse toward them. She glanced frantically at Billy's pistol and immediately discarded that option. If the man meant to kill them he had already had his chance.

Lee swung down from his horse and walked toward them. 'Is he all right?'

'Did you get that ambusher?' she asked angrily. Lee nodded. 'Good!' Vida hissed.

'Who was he, do you know?' Lee asked. From the descriptions he had gotten from Sheriff Archer, he was fairly sure that it was a man named Luke Skaggs, one of the bounty hunters. Why he would have chosen to assault these two young people was unclear to Saleen. With narrowed eyes he studied the youth with the dark curly hair as Vida continued to minister to him.

'We never saw him before,' Vida said. 'Maybe he wanted our water.'

That was possible, Lee considered. It was a ruthless act for such a small prize, but water had a high value out here. It was also possible that Luke Skaggs — if that was who it was — had been after a different prize.

'Are you OK?' Lee asked, crouching down beside the injured youth. He tilted his hat back, smiled and asked. 'What's your name?'

'B . . . en. Ben Minor,' Billy Gillis said, suddenly growing cautious. Who was this pale-eyed stranger?

'We've answered your questions,' Vida said, still holding Billy's head on her knee. 'Just who are you? How'd you happen to be here?'

Lee smiled again. He rose, telling her, 'I was just passing by, Vida. I thought I might ride on up and see

Cody if he was still on the ranch. Now . . . I don't know, seems he's got his usual amount of trouble circling. I suppose I'll leave it for another time.'

'You know Cody Minor?' Vida asked doubtfully.

'Sure,' Lee said, lying easily. 'I knew you, too, Vida. A long time ago. You were just a little kid when I saw you last.'

Vida said nothing. Billy had growled that he was all right, to leave him alone. Just a show of masculine toughness, but Vida let him have the small moment. Rising, Billy held his head with one hand, then bent stiffly to recover his pistol and took in a deep calming breath.

'We thank you, mister,' he said to Lee Saleen. 'He sure had us.'

'Next time, draw first,' Lee said with a wink, and Billy grinned painfully.

'We've got to be going,' Vida said impatiently.

Billy nodded, scooping up his hat. He was holding his wrist which was badly swollen, going black and blue. His fingers were stiffening. Vida would have to take the reins, he realized.

'Thank you again,' Billy said as he helped Vida clamber up on to the high bench seat of the freight wagon.

'Welcome,' was all Lee said, touching his hat brim. Then he turned and swung into his buckskin horse's saddle, riding away in the direction of Tucson as Vida started the wagon homeward.

'It's lucky that gent came along,' Billy said after a while.

'Was it?' Vida said, glancing at him. 'Did you notice that he never did give us his name.'

'There's a lot of men out West who don't wish to give up their names,' Billy pointed out. 'It doesn't matter, does it? He said that he knew Cody — that he even knew you.'

'Yes,' Vida said, her eyes on the trail ahead of the horses' ears, 'he did, didn't he? Said he knew me when I was just a little girl. Billy,' she told him, 'I've only been staying out here with Cody for a year and a half. Before that . . . well, some other people owned that ranch.'

Behind them on the trail, Lee Saleen watched as the wagon skirted the red ridge and continued on toward the dark hills. He did not know, for no one had an accurate description of him, but he thought the young man was probably Billy Gillis. And the girl, Vida? They had told him in Tucson, and she had confirmed, that she was Cody Minor's sister. He hadn't had the time to find out anything about Minor, but apparently he was known as a badman in this area. Did that mean that Pearly Gillis had thrown his lot in with another gang? Possible. If so, would Big Jack Corrigan be forced to hold his bounty hunters back until he could gather more recruits himself?

He sure wasn't going to find out just by sitting his horse and wondering.

Lee Saleen turned the buckskin's head northward and began following the ruts the wagon had left in the sand.

* ★ *

'Water wagon's coming, Jack,' Ken Wingate said, pointing southward. Jack Corrigan rose to his feet and peered that way.

'About time,' he growled. His patience was wearing thin. Dehydrated, and frustrated by Pearly Gillis's disappearance into the canyon, he felt thwarted and angry. Their horses stood lethargically, seeking poor forage which consisted of nothing more than dry bunch grass and mesquite beans, hardly enough for them to subsist on. Patience might be a virtue — at the time Jack had decided to sit and wait for the Gillis gang to reappear it had seemed so — but now it seemed a tactic gone badly wrong.

'Skaggs is taking his damned time about it,' Jack said.

'I don't see Luke,' Ken Wingate had to tell his bearded, red-faced leader.

'What do you mean! Of course Luke's there.'

'Don't see him,' Ken reiterated. 'Just

the kid and the girl.'

'Maybe he's in the wagon bed, holding his gun on them.'

'Don't see Luke's horse tied on behind,' Ken said doubtfully.

'Maybe those were shots we thought we heard,' young Tabor Corrigan commented.

'Yeah, and maybe the kid and the girl managed to take Luke Skaggs,' Jack Corrigan said scornfully. 'Don't make me laugh.'

'Stranger things have happened,' Ken Wingate muttered.

'Maybe . . . ' Tabor didn't finish his thought. What he was going to say was that maybe Luke Skaggs had had enough of the desert and decided to light out for the civilized world on his own. Probably that thought only reflected Tabor Corrigan's own ambition. His taste for bounty hunting had totally evaporated beneath the searing white sun.

'What do you want to do, Jack?' Ken Wingate asked.

'One way or the other, we need the water,' Big Jack said. Ken nodded. It was the answer he had expected. 'We take it,' Jack ordered.

The decision unexpectedly jarred Tabor's flimsy sense of right and wrong. Bounty hunting was authorized by the law. Robbery was robbery. He wanted to say something, would have, but his father's dark eyes flickered toward him once with enough silent authority to quell any objection he might have made.

Tabor dredged up enough courage to say, 'You can't let those people be hurt . . . I don't care to hurt them; there's no need for it.'

'If they got Skaggs . . . ' Ken Wingate put in ominously, and for the first time Tabor saw beneath the cheerful veneer of the tracker, saw into his hunter's heart as he had already seen into that of Skaggs. And into that of his father.

The three bounty hunters crept into the arroyo, slipping and sliding down the sandy bank, crossed the rocky bottom and bellied up the far slope to watch, rifles at the ready, as the water wagon rolled heavily toward them across the flats.

The wind still gusted from time to time, lifting veils of light sand. Tabor wiped his eyes clear and briefly closed them. Now what were they doing? They were going to behave like highwaymen themselves, no better than some of the men Big Jack had tracked down and killed for their crimes. Tabor was coming to the conclusion that his father, no matter what he had once seemed, was a man who saw himself not as a criminal, but one who felt that he was simply above the law.

The wagon was drawing nearer. Tabor Corrigan could hear the squeak of the hubs, the clink of trace chains, the horses' steady hoofbeats. He saw his father move, climb up out of the ravine with his rifle in one hand. Ken Wingate scampered up after him. With a suppressed groan, Tabor followed. The wagon ground to a halt at the approach of the armed men.

'What's this?' the youth on the bench seat of the wagon demanded. 'Who are you? What do you want?'

The girl who was driving was pretty, Tabor now saw. Dark-haired, slight, with hazel eyes and a full lower lip. She looked furious enough to spit. Tabor watched as his father approached the water wagon. Ken Wingate held his ground, rifle loose in his hands.

'I asked you what you wanted,' the kid with the dark curly hair said again. He looked as if he was ready to draw his Colt revolver; Tabor hoped not.

'Jack!' Ken Wingate shouted in warning. Corrigan glanced toward him and saw that the scout was pointing to the long flats beyond the wagon. 'There's a rider coming, Jack.'

Corrigan stepped aside to have a better look at the incoming horseman. He rode a stubby buckskin horse, wore a rust-red shirt and black jeans, black scarf and a pearl-gray Stetson hat.

'What'll we do?' Tabor asked nervously. The girl, after a backward glance fixed a poisonous gaze on Tabor Corrigan. Her look was harsh enough to cause him to turn his eyes down and away.

'Who's that trailing in?' Jack Corrigan asked the two seated on the water wagon.

'Ask him yourself,' Vida shot back. Twice in a day was too much. Why would the world not leave her alone! She had enough problems simply existing from day to day. Vida was so angry she couldn't have spoken more if she had chosen to.

Billy Gillis was looking over his shoulder as well, puzzled but relieved to see their benefactor again. He and Vida exchanged a wordless message as the lone rider drew nearer.

'What's the trouble, Ben!' Lee Saleen called as he slowed his buckskin and halted it beside the wagon. He had his Winchester across his saddlebow, held not menacingly but ready.

'These men stopped us,' Billy Gillis said.

'They did?' Lee said, lifting one eyebrow. 'Just why did you do that, boys?'

Thinking fast, Big Jack Corrigan answered, 'We been riding dry for a day and a half. We thought these folks could maybe sell us some water.'

'They can't,' Lee Saleen said softly. 'I might be able to help you, though. It's my water. The name's Sly. Richard Sly. These two are my niece and nephew. We've a little place up ahead.'

'You must know Pearly Gillis then,' Jack said as if it were only of casual interest to him. He had circled around the team of horses so that his line of fire could be directed at Lee Saleen if it came to that.

'Who?' Lee said too quickly. That was a mistake. A rancher up in those hills was unlikely not to know his neighbors. Vida quickly covered up for him.

'You remember, Richard — those men who rode to Cody Minor's place.'

'Them?' Lee tipped his hat back and scratched his head, nodding. 'I recall them, sure. Didn't get their names.' To Jack Corrigan he said, 'Couple of men rode up the valley yesterday afternoon. Didn't see them or their horses this morning. I stay out of my neighbors' affairs,' he added with the unspoken suggestion that Jack Corrigan do the same.

'What do you want for a barrel of water?' Big Jack asked, temporarily bluffed from the game.

Lee pondered, shrugged and said, 'Ten dollars. You take it down.'

'That's pretty high,' Jack said. Lee shrugged again.

'Five dollars in Tucson. Ten dollars here. My wagon, my hauling. Take it or leave it, I don't care which.'

Billy Gillis had to hide his smile. The stranger was playing it to the hilt, even haggling over the price of water. The bluff seemed to have worked, however. Jack Corrigan having no choice but to play out the game, and needing the water badly, forked over a ten-dollar gold piece which Saleen pocketed, and then gestured to Tabor and Wingate to clamber up on to the tall wagon and unstrap one of the heavy water barrels.

'Drop it and you've bought it anyway,' Lee Saleen said drily. Jack Corrigan's mouth tightened. He attempted one of his rare smiles and commented:

'You're a hard man, Sly.'

'You've no idea,' Lee Saleen answered flatly.

The two working men rolled the barrel down a heavy plank, stood it upright, slid the plank back into the wagon bed and stood uncertainly, waiting to see what Jack would do next. But what could he do? He just lifted a passing hand to Lee Saleen and turned deliberately away. Lee spoke to Vida.

'Let's take it home,' he said clearly. 'We've got some thirsty stock waiting.'

They started on toward the mouth of the canyon, and in minutes they were lost in its shadowy depths, leaving Big Jack Corrigan and his gang to stare hostilely after them. Lee Saleen trailed after the water wagon as Vida guided it along the rocky upslope farther into the chocolate-colored hills. It was still in the mountain pass, hot and windless. The wheels of the water wagon crushed stone beneath their iron rims. Vida guided the horses through the first of the elbow turns and drew up on a sheltered ledge no more than half an acre across. She waited, holding the leather ribbons as Lee walked his buckskin up beside her.

'What is it?' he asked.

'Where we're going, you can't follow,' she told him. 'We appreciate what you did, but . . . '

Lee held up a hand. Smiling, he answered, 'I know that, Vida. It's just that I can hardly turn back and ride out past those men. They'll know it was all a lie if I do that.'

'Who were they, anyway?' Billy Gillis asked. He was clutching his battered wrist. Ashen, obviously in pain, he was at once angry and confused. Lee did not answer him, although he knew full well from the descriptions he had been given that they were Big Jack Corrigan and his bounty hunters. Vida still held Lee's gaze, trying to make a decision.

'No,' she said at last, 'you can't go back that way. And you can't go ahead with us. Listen, whoever you are — there is a back trail out of the high valley. It's a rough trail, only wide enough for one horse, and very steep. I've only ridden it once. That was enough for me. It takes you down to more rough country, but no one will follow you. I'll show you the way once we've reached the high valley.

'But . . . ' she hesitated. 'You've got to promise to ride that way and leave us to our own business.'

'I've no wish to make trouble for you, Vida,' Lee told her. She held his gaze for another long moment, then made up her mind. She nodded, returned her attention to the horses, snapped the reins and started the wagon forward up the shadowed trail. Following the second elbow bend they emerged on to the barren flats of the high valley. To the north, Lee could make out the small structures where Pearly Gillis would be hiding, but he pretended to see nothing. Vida halted the team again.

'If you ride toward that split in the ridge, you'll see a scraggly old piñon pine. That marks the head of the trail. It might take a little searching, 'cause it doesn't look like much, but you'll find it. It's steep and its dangerous, but it'll get you down to the desert floor maybe ten miles north of Tucson. I just don't know what I'm going to tell Cody about you, about what happened to us.'

'Why tell him anything?' Lee asked quietly.

'There's the missing water barrel,' she replied.

'All right, then. Tell him the truth — you were stopped by some rough-looking men and you decided it was best to just sell them a barrel of water than to cause trouble. About me . . . well, I don't add much to the telling.'

Then Lee fished into his jeans,

withdrew the ten-dollar gold piece he had taken from Big Jack Corrigan and gave it to Vida. 'A little verification of your story,' he said.

'Cody still won't like it.'

'Maybe not. He can't have expected you to fight off three armed men, though. Just tell him you did your best under the circumstances. Besides,' Lee said thoughtfully, 'I've an idea that Cody Minor already knows that those men are down there waiting.'

Neither Billy nor Vida understood what the solitary man meant. As Lee touched his hat, turned and started his buckskin horse toward the distant trail Vida wondered aloud:

'Who is he? A lawman, do you think?'

'I don't know,' Billy said, though his heart gave a little jump. A lawman — of course. But then, if he was a lawman, why didn't the man calling himself Richard Sly arrest him? He had certainly had the opportunity. Why wasn't Sly wearing a badge, why didn't he identify himself to the men waiting down below? Vida's perception was a sound explanation for the rider's presence, but left too many questions unanswered.

'There's plenty of trouble in the air without worrying about him,' Vida said, starting the team homeward once more. 'Can you feel it, Billy?'

'Yes,' he admitted sorrowfully, 'I can. There's those men below . . . '

'And something between Pearly and Cody,' Vida said giving Billy Gillis a quick, agitated glance. 'I can sense that.' She added calmly, 'I don't have to guess, really; I know how all you robbers and thugs are. Someone is always looking for the main chance. I can read my brother like a book. He wants something that Pearly has.'

Billy only nodded, rubbing his battered wrist. He didn't want to confirm Vida's suspicions. Nor, he discovered with surprise, was he capable of lying to her, denying it. He was miserable once again, not the least because she had once again lumped

106

him with the rest of the rough men: a robber and a thug. He did not wish to be one; he wished he were someone that Vida Minor could admire. They were within sight of the ranch house when he managed to broach the thought he had been cultivating.

'Vida. Maybe you should get out of here. Off this mountain. Maybe . . . I could go with you.'

'Where would you take me, Billy Gillis? Just where would you take me,' she said, not mockingly, but with immense, weary sadness.

Rolling into the yard, they saw no one. From the house came the sounds of loud conviviality. The men were still at their whiskey. Something was near to breaking, Billy knew. Pearly would be ready to travel on with his horses rested and watered; Cody Minor would not be willing to let him leave, knowing that there was hidden booty stashed away on the desert. The two would either agree to a deal or it would come to shooting.

Billy did not believe that his cousin,

Pearly, was willing to pay any man's levy for the cost of a little water, hay and whiskey. It would come to shooting.

Feeling sick from the heat, from the long trek, the beating he had taken from Skaggs, tired of his own life, frustrated by his failure to impress Vida with his sincerity, Billy clambered down with some relief from the high wagon. He wondered if he dared to follow the nameless man down the long, aimless trail. Just ride away into an uncertain future.

Climbing down from the wagon, he helped Vida to the ground. For a moment — too long — he held her by her shoulders and said quietly: 'I mean it, Vida. About going away.' Ever so briefly her lips touched his cheek and then she twisted away from him, leaving him dazed with her moment of caring.

Billy hitched the horses loosely and removed his hat to wipe his forehead. The first crashing blow struck him before he saw trouble coming. Fists, elbows and knees clubbed him down and the world began a crazy, spinning motion as somewhere — far distant — Vida screamed.

6

Billy Gillis was being mauled by an unseen adversary. His face had been driven into the packed earth ground of the stable; his ribs were being hammered by clubbing fists. Billy twisted, writhed and fought back wildly until he was on his back, looking up into the flaccid, sadistic face of Virgil Spangler.

Spangler grinned with dark satisfaction and slammed his fist into Billy's jaw before he could roll his head away from the incoming blow. Flailing wildly, Billy was suddenly aware of an intruding shadow. Virgil had his arm cocked, ready to hit Billy again when a hand reached in, grabbed Virgil by his collar and yanked him away. Virgil was panting, his fists pawing wildly at the air as he was cast aside.

Standing over Billy now was Cody Minor, wearing a neat white shirt and black string tie, his eyes amused. 'You OK, boy?' he asked. Virgil sat to one side, knees drawn up, dull-eyed and seething with anger.

'What've we got here?' someone else asked, and Billy rolled his head to see Pearly, hatless, approaching. Cody Minor turned to respond.

'Couple of pups playin',' Cody said.

Rising to an elbow, Billy saw his cousin glance at Vida Minor who was standing nearby, her slender body rigid. Pearly nodded his understanding.

Virgil Spangler rose unsteadily and complained to Cody: 'He was mauling Vida. All over her. I saw it!'

'Vida can take care of herself,' Cody said coldly. 'If she can't — I'm her brother, and I take care of things, understand me, Virgil?'

Virgil intended to say something else, but the dark eyes of Cody Minor blunted his retort. He answered the gunman in a near whisper.

'Yes, sir, Mr Minor.' Then, still simmering, he clomped away, sparing

Billy a single poisonous glance across his shoulder.

'The kid's not too bright,' Cody Minor said to Billy, to Pearly or to himself. He leaned down, stuck out a hand and tugged Billy to his feet.

Billy stood swaying, then stepped back to lean against the side of the water wagon. Vida gave him one glance and then started off toward the house, followed by Pearly and Cody. Billy was left alone in the empty yard for a few minutes. He straightened, sucked in a deep breath and went to the lean-to stable where he rinsed his face and hands in the horse trough, wiping back his dark curly hair. He spent a few minutes visiting his dun pony, who alone seemed happy to see him. Beyond the lean-to Billy could see the sky slowly begin to redden as the sun heeled over toward the western peaks.

He hated this life! Hated everything about it, everything that was sure to come. He wanted nothing more than to leave, to follow the nameless man down the rugged trail to nowhere . . .

But there was Vida. He wanted *her* even more than his freedom, his safety, his life. Slowly, heavily, Billy replaced his hat and started back toward the ranch house.

He entered it to find Vida recounting the story of the men at the foot of the trail around mouthfuls of *pollo y arroz* — chicken and rice cooked by the heavy female Mexican cook whose name was Alicia. As far as Billy had been able to surmise, Alicia had been 'inherited' from the rancher who had formerly owned the tiny ranch. Dark, rotund, she went silently about her business with as little interaction as possible with the bandits. The cot where the dying man had been lying was empty now, Billy noticed. No one ever said a single word more about Woody Skyler and his passing. Such things were accepted. Maybe on some dark winter night someone might hoist a toast to old Woodrow, but for now he had simply vanished, as if he had never been. Billy couldn't help but wonder if that was to be his own fate.

'So,' Vida was saying, 'we sold them the barrel. What else were we supposed to do?'

'Wasn't much else to be done,' Cody agreed, although the look he gave Billy as he entered the room implied that he, Cody, had he been there, would have done a lot more. Drawn his ivory-handled Colt and given them hell.

Billy seated himself at the table and let Alicia serve him. He could hear her muttering under her breath in Spanish as she leaned her heavy body past his. Vida, he noted, had not mentioned the stranger who had come to their aid. 'Sly' was gone now, what difference could it have made? Nor did she mention the man who had first attacked them on the trail. The whipping Billy had taken from Virgil Spangler kept Billy from having to explain his earlier bruises. He was silently grateful to Vida for concealing that first encounter. He had the notion that the men at the table would have considered him a coward for not having drawn down on him as well.

'What did they look like?' Pearly Gillis asked, looking at his cousin. Billy told them as well as he could recall what the three waiting men had looked like. Pearly's habitual frown deepened.

'Ring a bell with you?' Cody Minor asked across the plank table.

'Sounds like Big Jack Corrigan and Ken Wingate,' Pearly muttered as he forked chicken and rice into his mouth.

'Corrigan. The bounty hunter?' Warren Spangler asked. 'I heard of him.'

Cody ignored the interruption. 'What do you want to do about it, Pearly?

'How many were they, Billy?' Pearly asked.

'Just three.'

'Three they saw,' Cody said, pushing his tin plate away and reaching for the whiskey bottle. 'Could be half a dozen, a dozen. Is it you they're after, Pearly?'

Grudgingly, Pearly admitted, 'Must be.'

A smile which never reached his lips shone in Cody Minor's eyes. He had his man now. The game had turned with the last card.

'It's tough, then,' Cody Minor said, glancing at the Spangler boys. 'Three of you against that bunch. You can't stay here. I don't want to be dragged into this, Pearly. Not unless there's something in it for us. Think the three of you can handle it? They'll have had plenty of time to take their positions. If I know Jack Corrigan, he has set his trap for any man leaving this valley.'

Pearly was slow in answering. He turned his coffee mug in slow circles, his mind turning with it. He was up against it, and he knew it. His voice crackling, he said:

'All right, Cody! You know what's up. What kind of deal do we make?'

'We ride with you.' Cody Minor gestured with two fingers toward the Spanglers. 'That makes it six against three — or so we hope. In return we want a split of whatever money you and

116

Ken have stashed down there. Don't look surprised, Pearly. I've known you a long time. I know how you do things. And Ken had no saddle-bags when he rode in. No sense in us trying to be cute with each other now. Let's make an honest deal. We'll help you shoot your way out for half of whatever it is you've got.'

'*Half?* You can go . . . '

'Half or we don't go anywhere. You will go. Out of here. This is not a safe refuge for anyone who just happens by. It took me a deal of trouble to establish this roost,' Cody said. 'I'm not going to shoot it out with the bounty hunters for nothing. I'd just have to give you up to them, Pearly. Use your common sense.'

'What's your plan, then?' Pearly asked, knowing that defeat was hovering over him.

'First, how much have you got?' Cody asked slyly.

Pearly glanced at Ken Wingate who reluctantly answered, 'Eighteen thousand, three-hundred.'

'Nine-thousand,' Cody said quietly. 'It's worth it, wouldn't you say?' he asked Virgil and Warren Spangler. Without waiting for an answer, he told Pearly:

'We don't need much of a plan,' Cody said confidently. 'They hold no warrants on me and the boys. We ride up to the bounty hunters, say howdy, tip our hats and gun them down.'

Pearly glanced at Billy. They shared the same thought.

As Cody would do to us once he gets his hands on the loot.

Still, Pearly had no choice but to go along with Cody's plan. The three of them weren't going to be able to fight their way through Big Jack's carefully planned ambush. With a show of gratitude, Pearly smiled, poured some liquor into his tin cup and hoisted it in the direction of Cody Minor.

'We've got a deal, Cody.'

Billy, watching the two thieves, knew that neither man had yet forfeited the game. Pearly wasn't going to give up

118

$9,000 willingly. Cody Minor knew that, and was probably already planning a way to snatch the entire amount while managing to stay alive.

Billy felt his stomach tighten and churn. He suddenly hated these men, one and all, his cousin, Pearly included. Vida was right about everything she said. They were all thugs and robbers, willing to gun each other down for a single gold piece, they were a blight on the fabric of civilization. He pushed his own plate away, unable to eat. He glanced at Vida, hoping for some encouragement, some promise of a better way, but there was none. She silently finished her food and rose to walk out into the yard. Billy's eyes followed her.

As did the hungry eyes of Virgil Spangler.

'At dawn, then,' Cody Minor was saying as he leaned back in his chair, his laundered white shirt so bright that it reflected the dancing firelight. 'Warren, Virgil and I ride up to Big Jack. Take the three of them out. You wait on our heels for anyone we might not know about popping up. You see anyone else we all swarm them. Right?'

'Sounds like the only way to do it,' Pearly Gillis agreed, taking another sip of his whiskey. 'The kid doesn't go, though,' he said, nodding at Billy.

'What do you mean!' Virgil Spangler shouted. 'What makes him special?'

'Nothing,' Billy Gillis said. 'I'll ride with you, Pearly,' he vowed.

'The hell you will!' Pearly shot back and they both rose to their feet. 'Look at you! You'd be no help, the shape you're in.'

Billy met his cousin's gaze with the heat of indignation, and then saw a curious and unexpected hint of concern in Pearly's deep-set eyes. As if his cousin was warning him to stay off the trail with them. Pearly's eyes shifted before Billy could be certain. Pearly was all business once again.

'All right with you, Cody?'

'It's all right with me,' Cody Minor

replied. He lifted his chin toward Vida. 'Someone should stay here to watch the girl anyway.'

Vida opened her mouth as if to counter that she could take care of herself, but perhaps she saw something similar to the fleeting glance Pearly had given Billy in her brother's eyes. She said nothing in response.

'Kid,' Cody Minor instructed Billy, 'you stay in the house with a rifle at the ready. You see anyone coming in but the five of us, start shooting.'

'All right, Cody,' Billy heard himself saying as if another man were speaking for him. His nerves had been rubbed raw; his head still ached from the beatings he had taken, but he knew that he would stand and fight to protect Vida no matter what.

Morning broke clear, silent and threatening. Pearly Gillis was the first man to the breakfast table. The others slowly appeared, all of them sleep-drugged, mouths filled with the sour memory of yesterday's whiskey. Pearly waited until everyone was finished eating before he looked to Cody, silently awaiting his orders.

'Let's trail on out,' Cody said quietly. 'The sooner it's done, the better.'

With that Cody strutted to the front door, flung it open and went out into the bright sunlight, the silver band on his hat gleaming, the white sun silhouetting his lean form. Pearly was more methodical, checking the loads in his pistol, in his long gun, stuffing his pockets full of extra cartridges before leaving the ranch house. Charley Stoddard hesitated, looking long at Billy before following in Pearly's wake. Billy thought that he knew what the look meant.

Stoddard had considered telling Billy where the stolen loot was concealed in case none of them made it back. He had not done so either because he was steadfast in his belief in his own immortality or because he thought Pearly would not like it. As it was, Pearly must have concluded that with only him and Charley knowing where the bank's money was hidden, Cody Minor would not be inclined to gun them down out of hand.

As Pearly had said: it was all about the money, after all.

Warren and Virgil Spangler shouldered past Billy as he stood in the doorway, watching the outlaws mount their horses. Of these two Virgil was a buffoon, but that did not keep him from having a deadly streak in him. His hatred for Billy had already been demonstrated. Real or imagined, Virgil considered that he had a claim on Vida and that Billy was standing in his way.

Vida stood beside Billy as the riders swung on to their mounts and left the ranch yard, their horses stirring up wavelets of fine dust. She said:

'They won't all be coming back.'

'No,' was all Billy could find for an answer.

'It's the money!' Vida said with sudden vehemence. She turned her back and stalked away, swiping the silverware and plates from the table before Alicia's astonished eyes. 'That's all it is ever about with you thugs and robbers,' she shouted, using her favorite phrase. 'Nobody cares if anyone is killed. Do you know why, Billy?' she asked in a softer tone, and continued:

'It is because they have no honor beyond the gun. They're all out for the main chance. They don't form friendships — not in any real sense. The other man is always expendable. So long as they profit from it.'

It seemed to Billy that Vida was ready to sob, to cry for men that she alone cared for, but she swept out of the room before the emotion was fully expressed.

Billy busied himself helping Alicia clean the floor and the table. Alicia mopped and muttered, sang and cursed as she worked. Billy was out of curses. He had used them all up in the past few days. The sun rose higher and he sagged into the corner chair, his eyes blank and haunted with the futility of it all.

Big Jack Corrigan had not been idle. He couldn't afford to be.

'The tables have turned on us,' Jack was saying to Ken Wingate as the two squatted on their heels, sharing coffee from a pot boiling over a low-burning fire. Young Tabor Corrigan stared at the brightening western sky, hardly hearing the two bounty hunters. 'It's time to reorganize,' Corrigan said.

'What are you thinking, Jack?' Wingate asked.

'Look — Luke Skaggs is gone,' Big Jack said intently. 'We've got to assume he's dead. That leaves the three of us. We know that there's six or seven men up in the hills at the least. I've got no idea who that pale-eyed rider was, the one calling himself Richard Sly, but we've got to believe that he's gotten the word to Pearly Gillis that we're down here waiting.'

'Must figure that,' Wingate agreed thoughtfully.

'They'll have made plans to hit us,' Jack said, finishing his coffee, throwing the dregs on to the tiny fire. 'They won't like that trapped feeling of us being down here. The trouble is the men Pearly met up with must know this country better than we do. We can't sit here and wait to be flanked.'

'No,' Ken Wingate answered. The buckskin jacketed scout rose and tossed the remainder of his coffee into the fire as well. 'It's coming on to first light. They'll come hunting for us. What do you suggest, Jack?'

'We've got to take the high ground, Ken. Find ourselves a neat little place and dig in. And get ready for a turkey shoot.'

Tabor Corrigan, listening distantly, felt a shiver crawl through him, rise from his spine to the nape of his neck. The term was unsettling. *Turkey shoot* — they were going to find a vantage point from which to lay an ambush, shooting down every man who passed their position whether they had a warrant on him or not. All of it could be explained later, if anyone even asked. After all, the West would be rid of a few more outlaws, so what was the difference?

When Ken Wingate restated their situation it seemed to make more sense, though it was no more palatable.

'They'll sure as hell be looking to kill us, Jack. We strike first — that's the only answer.'

Jack nodded. 'Let's saddle up then. Tabor,' Big Jack said to his son, 'when we get into that canyon, keep your eyes ahead and behind. You see anything moving, even a shadow, go to shooting. Better safe than sorry.' To Ken Wingate, Big Jack Corrigan said with rough confidence, 'There's those who've tried us before, aren't there, Ken! Tried it — but we're the ones who are still above ground.'

They saddled their ponies then and started up the long rocky trail into the broken hills to look for their killing ground.

Billy Gillis had seen to his pony. The dun horse, without complaint, stood quietly in the lean-to. A normally quiescent, docile animal, still it must have wondered why its human friend was not exercising him, why they were not on some long and magical new trail.

Billy leaned against a pole upright, his hat tilted back. Automatically, he flexed his fingers and rubbed his swollen wrist. His mind was not on the exercise but on Vida. Only on Vida. What had he gotten himself into? What sort of life had circumstances dragged her into? She had paid him scant attention that morning. Distancing herself from him made Billy feel that perhaps he was actually worthless, a thug! No clever remark of his brought a smile to her lips. No pleasantry lightened her gloom. They simply waited. Waited for the gunshots, waited to see who would return alive.

With a sudden surge of decision, Billy straightened, tossed away the bit of straw he had been toying with and marched steadfastly toward the ranch house. He stamped in so forcefully that Vida glanced up with shock from her seat at the long table. Her hazel eyes were wide, her lip trembled slightly as if he were some unexpected assailant.

Billy stopped in his tracks, began to speak, hesitated and sat opposite Vida, his forearms folded on the table.

'We could go. Just leave,' he said with urgency and pleading mingled in his voice.

'We could . . . ?' Vida tried to laugh but could not manage it in the face of the young man's sincerity.

Billy said: 'That man — that Richard Sly — he just rode away from all of this, didn't he? Down the hidden trail. Vida,' he said imploringly, 'we can do the same thing. This is no life for you . . . or for me.'

Then Vida laughed. It was not a mocking laugh, but one of astonishment. She said, 'Billy, I ride away with you? Why, you can't even take care of yourself!'

Billy spread his hands pleadingly; Alicia had appeared in the kitchen door; but he paid her no attention. 'Maybe I haven't shown you much, Vida. Every time I get into a fight I get the worst of it, that's for sure! You may be right, Vida — but you can take care of me.' His voice dropped to a whisper as he reached for her hand. 'And that will give me all of the strength I need to take care of *you*.'

She took his hand tentatively, squeezed two of his fingers. Her lips parted, she began to respond.

And the shattering echoes of gunfire racketed up the canyon as a flurry of violence erupted in the broken hills.

7

'Richard Sly' had risen with the dawn light, seen to his buckskin horse, made a small pot of coffee, gnawed on salt biscuits and beef jerky and waited, knowing that this day would bring the roar of guns and the cries of bloodied men. More, he knew that there was little he could do to stop it.

It remained a fact of law that Jack Corrigan had every right to use whatever force he deemed necessary to take down Pearly Gillis and his men. The warrants, after all, did expressly read 'dead or alive'. No matter what Lee Saleen thought about the law as it was now interpreted, he could not legally interfere with a sanctioned enterprise. He had known since day one that it would come to this — he could not intervene in an authorized extermination, no matter how odious he might feel it to be.

He couldn't, in truth, even be sure that his sensibilities were in the right place. Pearly Gillis, after all, was a well-known killer. Cody Minor, from what Saleen had heard, was no better, but there was no warrant that Lee was aware of out for Cody's arrest. This was Lee Saleen's justification for interfering in this slaughter.

Cody Minor and any of his gang were protected by law from being hunted by the bounty killers. If Big Jack Corrigan chose to shoot these men down indiscriminately — no matter what they might be suspected of — then Lee had every right to arrest Jack Corrigan to halt his wild excesses.

All of that was easier said than done. No intellectual exercise was going to bring the well-armed men with blood in their eyes to an amicable solution. Their way of doing business was to conclude disputes with a Colt .44. Lee had no illusions about his prospects of ending this before men, perhaps many men, had died. He did not understand all of the dynamics in play, but he knew that money was involved, a lot of money.

And *it was all about the money.*

The first shots rang out before Lee Saleen had finished saddling his buckskin horse.

Leaving his gear behind, he mounted hurriedly and spurred his buckskin toward the sound of the guns.

* * *

It was Warren Spangler who took the first bullet. Trapped in the narrow draw, the bounty hunters firing from the stacked yellow boulders surrounding the trail, the robbers scattered, racing their ponies for cover. Only Cody Minor was quick enough to fire back, but three scattered shots from his ivory-handled pistol did little but spray rock chips into the air. Warren, slammed from his saddle by a slug to his chest, managed to rise again. As his brother sped past him, Warren made the mistake of trying to grab the tail of

133

the fleeing bandit's black horse. Instead of being a ticket out of the cross-fire, the horse's hoofs finished what the shot had not. An iron-shod hoof from the black pony sledge-hammered into Warren's skull, killing him instantly as Virgil, heedless of all but his own skin, raced on, flagging his horse with his reins.

Pearly Gillis had nearly reached the safety of a low granite bench when he felt his Appaloosa stagger and begin to roll, shot from under him. He was dumped roughly to the stony earth, rolled twice and got briefly, madly to his feet to fire back wildly at the bounty hunters. His bullets too struck only rock, and leaping across his downed pony now in its death run, Pearly dove toward the shelter of the gray granite ridge.

The rocks, shattered by the vagaries of harsh climate and the roots of dead pinons, which stood in a dismal row behind Pearly, afforded plenty of protection if a man kept his head buried in the sandy soil, but you don't win a fight by hiding and waiting for the other soldiers to run out of ammunition.

'Pearly!' a voice shouted from behind Gillis and he briefly shifted the muzzle of his Colt that way before recognizing that it was Cody Minor who had called to him.

'Can you cover us?' Cody yelled. 'I've got Charley with me.'

'Come on ahead,' Pearly said. 'Keep low, Cody.'

Pearly thrust his Colt over the rim of the rocks and fired with random rapidness at the bounty hunters hidden in the rocky rise beyond the trail. Charley Stoddard reached the rocky shelter first, throwing himself toward cover, landing on his belly beside Pearly. Cody arrived on Charley's heels. Firing on the run, he hit no target but drew an answering shot from a Winchester that struck far too close to their heads.

'Damnit all!' Cody Minor said

sharply as he leaned against the rocks with their thin veneer of yellow lichen, thumbing fresh cartridges into the cylinder of his revolver. 'I knew that old bastard Corrigan would reposition his boys.'

'It's not your fault, Cody,' Pearly Gillis said with surprising empathy. 'We had to make a move. If we'd stayed in the ranch house Big Jack would have sat there sniping at us until we were all dead or starved out.'

Cody nodded grimly, slammed the cylinder of his ivory-handled Colt shut and peered up over the gray granite bench. He was getting to like Pearly Gillis after all, he thought. It would be a damned shame to have to kill him and his men after they showed him where the bank loot was hidden.

'Where are those two pups of yours?' Charley Stoddard asked Cody. 'I don't see them.'

'You won't see Warren again,' Pearly told him. 'He took a killing shot. Virgil, I don't know.'

'Virgil won't run,' Cody Minor said with a confidence he didn't feel. If he had not run . . . then where was he? It was to be hoped that Virgil Spangler had survived and would find a way to flank Big Jack and his bounty hunters.

'Could you tell how many guns are up there?' Pearly asked Stoddard, but the scout shook his head.

'I thought only a couple, three, Pearly, but I don't know for sure.'

'Could be that there are others down below,' Cody said. 'Maybe the shots will bring them on the rim. Maybe Big Jack told them just to hold their position and see if he could flush us out of the canyon and back out on to the desert.'

'I don't like this a bit,' Pearly muttered. Charley Stoddard had his twin pistols out, ready for a fight, but the gun battle had settled into what promised to be a long stand-off, with the first man to show his head the first to go. Pearly wiped the perspiration from his eyes and asked Cody, 'Any ideas?'

'No. Did you lose your horse, Pearly?'

'Shot from under me.'

'My bay ran off as well. Charley?'

'My gray's back in the pines, though I can't see what good he's doing us there.'

Four, five, a dozen rifle shots were rapidly fired from across the trail and the outlaws buried their heads again as rock chips splintered off the face of the bench.

'Three rifles,' Charley muttered inconsequentially.

'Virgil will find a way to get behind them,' Cody Minor said. 'The boy's not bright, but he hunts like he's got Indian blood in him. He knows what to do.'

'Maybe Billy will ride in,' Charley commented.

'They'd cut him down,' Pearly said. 'Besides, I told the kid to stay put at the ranch house. He'll stay put.'

Cody turned his back to the rocks and sat down, wiping his face which was drenched in perspiration. The desert sun was riding high in the pale sky now. Cody said, 'It's a long time to nightfall, boys. Hell of a long time to be pinned down without water.'

'I feel like going after them,' Charley said savagely, but Pearly Gillis touched the sleeve of Charley Stoddard's buck-skin shirt.

'You know that's what they want, Charley. For us to get all wild-eyed and charge up those rocks.'

'I know it, Pearly,' Charley said with weary resignation. 'I know it. There's nothing to do but wait this out, but I am going to make someone pay for it if I am forced to sit here all day. This damned, thirsty heat, Pearly — I'm not sure it's much better than dying.'

★ ★ ★

All hell had broken out along the high valley trail. Lee Saleen could smell gunsmoke in the air even as far as he was from the action when he crested the grassless ridge, dismounted and bellied to the rim of the hill to look down at the site. From his position, his first glance showed him three men bunkered down behind a gray granite bench. It took a while longer for him to make out the other men, further away, but the glint of sunlight on their rifle barrels gave them away. They, too, were unable or unwilling to mount an attack. Between the two groups lay the still form of a horse and a dead man, an outlaw, although Lee could not make out who he might be.

'This is a situation, isn't it?' he muttered to himself. His buckskin horse lifted its patient head, glanced at him and then began foraging again.

Who, Lee wondered, did he help here? Who did he attack? The bloody bounty killers, the money-mad outlaws? Yet to watch indecisively went against his grain. He told his uninterested horse, 'I guess there's nothing much to do, except to watch and arrest the last man standing.'

Movement to the east attracted his gaze. Someone rushing to aid his friends? No, the rider was whipping his pony furiously away from the battle. Frowning, Lee watched the man. Again, at this distance he was unable to identify the rider or even form a rough description of him in his mind.

Lee supposed that it did not matter. If the man had given it up, so much the better. He returned his scrutiny to the group below him who now found themselves in a stalemate from which the only escape was death.

★ ★ ★

The sun, though riding high, was still low enough to glare through the window of the ranch house where Billy Gillis stood, rifle in hand, squinting out across the barren yard. Not five minutes earlier he and Vida had heard a flurry of shots, followed a minute later by another barrage. Vida, seated in the barrel chair in the shadowed corner of the room, hid her eyes behind her hands.

'It's all over,' she said quietly.

'We don't know what has happened,' Billy said without shifting his eyes from the long yellow-gray expanse of valley beyond the window.

'No matter! It's all over,' Vida said, lowering her hands. 'It was only a matter of time. Only a matter of time for you as well.'

At the approach of shuffling foot-steps, Billy turned his head to see the heavy cook, Alicia, coming into the room. She had a rolled blanket in her hands and wore a straw hat. Beyond her, Billy could see that the kitchen had been scrubbed, the dishes washed and put away.

'I go,' Alicia said sadly.

'You don't have to do that,' Billy told her. 'Wait and talk to Cody.'

'I go.'

'Alicia!' Vida tried. The Mexican woman just shook her head heavily and said again:

'I go. I have *burro*. This is a place so *malo*, it's no place for anyone. I go now.'

They could tell by the sadness in her eyes, the set of her face, that there was no sense in trying to talk her out of her decision. Besides, Billy Gillis realized as he stepped aside to make room for her to pass toward the door, she was right: this was a bad place, a very bad place to be. Billy lifted the bar to the door, opened it for Alicia, then closed it again behind her.

Billy glanced out the window once more and then walked slowly to where Vida sat, hands clasped between her knees. Halting before her, he stood, rifle in both hands, trying to find a way to frame his words.

'They won't be coming back, Vida,' he said at last. 'Not all of them. All hell has broken loose. Alicia knows that. She knows when it's time to pull up stakes.'

'It's not *her* brother down there,' Vida said without looking up.

'No. I know you're concerned about

Cody, but what can he offer you anyway?'

'He took me in when no one else would!' Vida said, now raising her angry eyes.

'I know that,' Billy answered. 'I don't know much about Cody. I admit it. But you can't have any kind of life at all if you remain here.' He rushed on before she could interrupt. 'And I don't believe that he would ever want you harmed. I saw the look that passed between you two. He cares for you. But you're in a dangerous position here, Vida. You have to realize that! Cody won't be able to protect you for ever. Not with the men, the business he surrounds himself with.'

'What are you telling me? To just ride away and leave him to his fate!' Vida rose, stabbed at her light brown hair with her fingers and walked to the window. Nothing stirred . . .

'Yes,' Billy said quietly. There was no malice toward Cody Minor in his voice, no anger and no fear — except for Vida.

'Ride out with me, Vida,' he pleaded. 'There has to be a better life for you somewhere.'

'With you!' she asked heatedly.

'If you choose it,' he answered. He touched one of her shoulders, let his hand fall away and then turned his back on the distraught woman.

'And what kind of man are you who would ride off and leave your cousin to his fate!' Vida asked sharply.

'The kind who knows that Pearly got along without me before I persuaded myself to ride with him, that whatever befalls him I am not the cause of it.' Billy half-smiled and shook his head. 'The kind who knows that the outlaw life is not for me and that if Pearly continues his reckless ways he will get himself killed. And if I follow in his tracks, I will meet the same fate.' Carefully he added:

'I am the kind of man, Vida, who would travel anywhere with you and try to please you, who will never put you in the path of violence again.'

'Billy . . . ' Vida could not finish her thought. She looked to the curly-haired young man, glanced toward the window, listening for the gunfire which was certain to ring out again, announcing the deaths of the badmen. If not Cody's death, then Pearly's. If not them, then that of Charley Stoddard or the Spangler boys. She looked toward the cot where Woody Skyler had spent his last anguished hours, dying years before his time because of the wild life they all lived.

She did not lift her eyes when she spoke again. Her words were as quiet as the wings of a dove.

'Let's go, Billy. Out of here. Away to what ever might await us.'

Billy Gillis nodded, stepped to her and held Vida briefly in his arms. Neither was alerted by the cautious footsteps on the plank porch until the boot slammed against the barred door, banging it open. When Virgil Spangler burst through the doorway, his pistol leveled, he shouted out in rage:

146

'At it again, are you! Throw that rifle aside, Gillis or I'll kill you where I stand. Vida is mine and I'm taking her no matter how I have to do it.'

8

'Where's Cody!' Vida shouted, stepping away from Billy.

'How the hell should I know! Why would I care?' the wild-eyed man asked.

'You . . . just ran out on them?' Vida asked in disbelief.

'They got themselves into a situation they're not going to be able to fight their way out of. My brother Warren is dead. I wasn't going to join him. The bounty hunters have them pinned down. Cody and Pearly might be handy with their guns, but they've had it this time.'

Vida asked again, 'And you ran off and *left* them?'

Virgil Spangler glanced at Billy and said, 'It looks to me like that's exactly what you were planning on doing, Vida.'

'I'm not a man,' Vida said pityingly,

'and it seems that neither are you, Virgil.'

'Shut up!' Virgil said in a growl that was the product of a rage neither Billy or Vida could understand. Perhaps he did feel shame at having deserted his gang in the heat of battle; perhaps his anger was triggered by the knowledge that Vida preferred the young, curly-headed stranger, Billy Gillis, to him.

Vida took a step toward him, her small fists clenched and Virgil back-handed her hard across the face, slamming her against the wall. Billy choked on a savage oath and threw himself at Virgil Spangler. The young, pale-eyed outlaw shot him as he charged.

The round from Spangler's .44 caught Billy in the shoulder with the force of a sledgehammer and spun him around. Billy reached out toward Vida, lost his balance and slammed face first into the rough plank floor, his body shaking wildly, then going still, bleeding life on to the ranch house floor.

★　　★　　★

The shot from the ranch was so distant that Big Jack Corrigan didn't even hear it above the rush of the heated tormenting wind that swept across the canyon. His planned ambush had begun well enough. One of the outlaws' horses had gone down; a bandit lay dead against the dusty earth below the stacked yellow boulders where Jack, Tabor and Ken Wingate had concealed themselves. The sun was blistering hot; touching the steel of his Winchester repeater was akin to picking up a branding iron bare-handed.

Perspiration rolled into his eyes; his mouth was parched. The memory of the shared luxury when they had opened that water barrel had faded long ago.

'They can't stay hunkered down there for ever,' Ken Wingate said, tugging at his shirt front to let a little air circulate. 'All this requires is a little patience, Jack.'

Big Jack Corrigan, however, was not a patient man. He had the bandits where he wanted them, but he was unable to finish the deal. The bounty hunters' horses had been picketed atop the bluff behind the stacked boulders, but it did not matter. They could do no more with horses under them than they could this way. Jack cursed, mopped his forehead again and settled in among the sun-baked boulders.

Tabor Corrigan glanced at his father, wondering at his doggedness. Hitting the trail with the bounty hunters young Tabor had imagined would be a far different enterprise — perhaps circling a band of thieves around their night campfire, tying their hands and leading them back to be tried as the hunters, praised and slapped on the back, were paid their rewards.

The last three days had been nothing more than a lingering hell. Even now, with their quarry in sight, there was no forseeable end to this desert nightmare. How did Big Jack manage to start each new pursuit, to forge ahead no matter the consequences? Tabor had to wonder if some dark force he knew nothing of drove his father. Tabor's eyes were on an iridescent beetle that scuttled this way and that across the boulder where his arms rested. The bug moved erratically, confused or unable to stand the heat on its feet, unable to understand how to avoid it.

This is it, Tabor told himself. No matter what happened, this was his first and last bounty. A simple hard-working cowhand went through less hell than this. He might not make as much money, but every day was not a kill or be killed proposition. The hell with the money.

'The hell with this,' Tabor heard Ken Wingate mutter. 'This can't go on, Jack. You're right, patience isn't going to get it done. After dark they'll slip away and we'll be lucky to pick up their trail again. We've got to take it to them.'

'Do you have an idea of how to do that?' Jack shot back with ill-temper.

'Not a good one,' Wingate admitted with a shake of his head, 'but we've got to break the stalemate. You know that.'

Jack was silent for a long minute, glancing up the rocky slope behind them. Sliding down the jumble of boulders had proved to be no problem. Going up, with men shooting at them, was: a large problem. Wingate tugged at his long, thin beard thoughtfully and finally offered:

'If you can keep them pinned down, Jack, I might be able to reach the ponies. I might be able to circle the outlaws and get into those pine trees behind them. Then it becomes a whole new game.'

'It's a long climb, Ken. And a long ride around.'

'I know it,' Wingate answered soberly. 'I'd rather try it than keep this up. Come nightfall they'll slip out one by one anyway. Likely they'll decide to split up, and there goes the bounty.'

Jack didn't like the suggestion, but Ken Wingate did have a point. It should

153

be finished off here. He had no desire to ride back out on to the flat desert, trying to pursue Pearly and his men once more. This, most likely, was their best opportunity to take the outlaws down.

'If you think you've got a chance,' Jack said, surveying the rugged stack of boulders.

'I always think I've got a chance,' Wingate said with a starched smile. 'Else I wouldn't ride with you in the first place. I'm going, boys. Keep your sights on Pearly's crew, and keep your rifle barrels hot.'

★   ★   ★

Lee Saleen sat cross-legged on the rise opposite Big Jack's stronghold, still considering whether or not to take a hand in the deadly game being played out below him. He saw no way that he could bring events to a satisfactory conclusion. That being so, he would have to be content to watch the actors play out their savage roles in the contest.

He heard a shot echo up the canyon and shifted his pale eyes toward the distant ranch house. A single shot. Who had it been fired at and who had pulled the trigger? He could not be sure at that distance, but he believed that the man he had seen escaping the gun battle had ridden to the ranch where, so far as he knew, only the girl remained. The shot made no sense, but as he had already realized, there was more at play here than he knew.

Still mediating darkly on that, he was roused by the sound of thunderous gunfire. A dozen shots, fifty. Saleen could see a man scrambling up the boulders behind Jack Corrigan's position, clawing at the rocks, dragging himself up the sun-blistered rough yellow stones toward the bluff over-shadowing the battlement.

The men in the rocks laid down a fierce covering fire at the outlaws hidden behind the low gray granite bench. Bullets flew in the other direction as well, but these were carelessly aimed, none of the Gillis-Minor gang apparently being willing to rise up and take accurate aim at the fleeing man.

Still bullets peppered the rocks around the escaping bounty hunter as he reached the crest, rolled on to the flats and ran in a crouch toward a trio of picketed horses the bank robbers could not see from their position low in the valley.

'I'll be damned,' Lee murmured, as the bounty hunter swung on to a pony's back and heeled it into a run, for it was now obvious that the man had no intention of fleeing to the south, but to ride north and west and circle the band of outlaws who were pinned down. Whoever he was, the man had some heart, Lee had to admit.

Lee watched. He waited. He wished he had not abandoned his meager supplies back at his campsite, for he was growing hungry again. He felt burdened by the shadow of regret now darkening his mood. He knew full well that he was going to have to kill a man, maybe more than one, before this day was done. None of these — bounty killer or outlaw — was the sort to surrender to him. They had proved that with their recklessness.

Not for the first time that morning, Lee Saleen found himself wishing that he, himself, had chosen another path in this world.

★ ★ ★

The conversation among the outlaws as the barrage of covering fire from the rocks above came to a stop was excited and contentious.

'He got up,' Charley Stoddard said uneasily, meaning the bounty hunter who had reached the rim of the bluff. 'I think it was Wingate. Did anyone tag him?'

'Where's he going?' Pearly asked, sagging back against the granite bench again. 'Do you think they have more men down below on the flats?'

'The shots would have brought them already,' Cody Minor said, thumbing fresh cartridges into the magazine of his Winchester. 'Wingate is going to try to circle us. Where in hell is Virgil? He could stop him if he's out there.'

'Run away,' Pearly said bitterly. 'That's where Virgil is.'

'Virgil doesn't run!'

'He's sure not doing any fighting.'

'Maybe the first volley got him.'

'Maybe you're only worried about him because you've lost one Spangler and now you won't have much of a chance of jumping us and taking the bank money, Cody!' Pearly answered angrily, blurting out a thought that had long been on his mind.

Cody's hand dropped to his holstered ivory handled pistol and a cold, snakelike gleam settled into his eyes.

'I wouldn't try it, Cody,' Charley Stoddard said easily. 'Now or any time.' His rifle muzzle was lowered to the level of Cody's belt buckle.

'All right, all right!' Cody said. 'This isn't going to get us out of this fix. Sure I had designs on the money. I still take you at your word, Pearly, that you'll agree to a split. But let's get out of here first!'

* * *

After an initial burst of speed, Ken Wingate slowed his horse to a walk. The animal was again thirsty. The sun flared hotly against the pale sky. The ground was rough. Ken did not know the lie of the land, and he had to swing his pony carefully back and forth atop the bluff, searching for a way down. He halted his weary mount and surveyed the land, tugging at his long, narrow beard as he was prone to do in moments of reflection.

Bothering him more than the brutal desert conditions, more than finding a way to circle the outlaw stronghold was the knowledge that there were still two members of the Pearly-Minor gang unaccounted for. The spate of gunfire might have brought them on the run, but he could see no horsemen across all of the long, barren valley below. Still he rode cautiously. A man didn't last long in this business without using some caution. There were times when rashness was essential — like scaling those rocks to reach his horse, but there were others when a moment's careful consideration could add years to your life.

The trail down, when Wingate eventually found one, was rock-strewn, narrow and steep. Wingate shook his head, silently apologized to his horse and spurred it forward. The bluff loomed only 150 feet or so above the valley floor, but the ride down was as perilous as any he had made for a long time. The horse's hoofs skated over loose debris and the animal quivered under him. Ken gnawed at his lip and continued on, telling himself that there were men depending on him.

Reaching the flats, Ken let his

shuddering horse stop and blow. He could make out the stand of scraggly pinon pines from where he now rested. Although he didn't like the idea of crossing the open flats on a dog-tired pony, he figured he could make it.

With a little luck.

Then — with a little luck — he would be into the concealment of the dusty pine trees and he should be able to Indian-up on the concealed outlaws and scatter or kill them each and every one with his long gun. Ken Wingate had no feelings one way or the other about gunning them down. There was a bounty on them. When the government or local ranchers put a bounty on wolves or cougars, the men who hunted them down for a price didn't spend a lot of time worrying about a sheep-killing puma's feelings. You did a job; they paid you for it, that was all.

Riding at a walk still, his eyes flickering from point to point across the valley, Ken found himself entering the wind-twisted, weather broken pines and he released a long-held breath. He had made it, apparently unseen by the enemy — which was how he thought of the bandits. An enemy force. Not wanting to take a chance on the horse nickering or breaking branches underfoot, Wingate swung down and tethered his pony loosely to a low-hanging branch. His hat, he hung on the pommel of his saddle. He unsheathed his Winchester and started on through the heated tangle of shadows.

'I'm getting too old for this,' he thought, not for the first time.

But the work was well worth it when it came time to be paid. This bunch was worth $1,200. Luke Skaggs's share would be added to the split now that he had vanished. If the bank's money could be recovered, there was usually ten per cent of that added to the reward. Wingate's share would be enough for him to take two, three years off if he so chose. And he was thinking that that was just what he might do this time. He and Jack Corrigan had ridden a lot of trails together, but lately Big Jack seemed to have become too impulsive, more likely to rush into trouble than previously. Not good attributes for a bounty hunter. Yes, Ken Wingate was thinking as he stalked his prey among the tangle of trees, the pungent pine scent and crisscrossed shadows surrounding him: only this once more.

There was an abrupt flurry of gunfire from below and answering shots from Jack and Tabor in the boulders above. Wingate frowned in puzzlement, but assumed the shots to be simply random in nature.

Weaving on through the trees he came upon a position where he could clearly see the bank robbers below him, and he went to his belly against the dry pine needles that were scattered heavily across the hillside. Peering down to where the bandits were attempting to conceal themselves behind the lichen-covered granite bench, Ken took careful aim, calculating for windage and drop and opened up with his Winchester.

★ ★ ★

'He's had time to get into the trees,' Charley Stoddard had told the others minutes earlier.

'Make you nervous, does it?' Cody Minor asked derisively.

'Damn right,' Charley answered, mopping his forehead with his shirt front. 'That was Ken Wingate, not some greenhorn.'

'Think you could find him up there, Charley?' Pearly Gillis asked.

'I think someone had better give it a try, Pearly,' Stoddard answered with some concern. 'If I can reach the verge of the pines, I can lay for him.'

'All right,' Pearly Gillis answered. 'Give it a try. We can't have someone in those trees with a rifle at our backs.'

Charley Stoddard nodded, cast his hat aside and rose into a crouch. He glanced at the two gunmen who were to cover his dash toward the forest, paused for a three-count, nodded and took off at a run, zigzagging his way across the open ground toward the piñons. Among the boulders, Jack Corrigan and Tabor, unprepared for the move and the following barrage of covering fire from the outlaws' rifles, managed to take only half a dozen ill-aimed shots at the running man in the buckskin shirt.

Achieving the verge of the woods, Charley Stoddard leaned against the trunk of a gnarled pine and took in a series of deep, restoring breaths. He heard motion ahead of him and went to one knee, leaving a round into the breech of his Winchester. Then he smiled and relaxed. The sounds had come from his own tethered gray horse. The animal recognized him, whickered and pawed the ground impatiently. Charley lowered his rifle and approached his horse through the maze of tree shadows.

★   ★   ★

Ken Wingate heard the horse nicker, but mistakenly took it for his own mount. He remained bellied down on the pine-needle-strewn rise behind the granite bench where the outlaws were hiding. Had he arrived just a moment earlier, he would have seen Charley Stoddard crossing the open ground below, but he had not seen the plainsman dart into the depths of the pines.

His attention was now fixed on the iron sights of his rifle. Peering along the Winchester's barrel, he settled the front bead into the V of the rear sight. He triggered off his first shot, using the white shirt of Cody Minor as his target. The following echo racketed up the hillslope. It was a long shot, but a good one.

Cody Minor had been sitting with his back against the granite bench, thumbing his last six loads into his rifle. He heard the shot a split second after the bullet from Charley Stoddard's rifle ripped through his chest. With puzzlement, Cody

166

touched his breast and said:

'Pearly . . . I think I've had it.'

Pearly Gillis rolled and twisted away as two more shots sang off the face of the granite stronghold. He could see the puffs of smoke rising from the forest verge, and as Stoddard's third shot ripped through Pearly's thigh, he screamed out angrily and began levering bullets through the barrel of his own rifle.

His success was no more than could be expected when firing wildly at a puff of smoke. His shots went nowhere near Stoddard, but Charley's fourth bullet crashed into Pearly's ribs, sending him sprawling to lie inert against the hot gravel-covered earth, blood leaking from his wounds.

Ken Wingate smiled grimly, and — truthfully — a little proudly as he sat up in a cross-legged position, surveying the two motionless outlaws below him. He looked to the pile of stacked yellow boulders beyond the two dead men and lifted his arm, pumping his rifle twice in the air. It was doubtful that Big Jack could have seen him at that distance, but the triumphant gesture made Ken feel better.

'Wingate?' the voice behind Ken said quietly, and Ken Wingate spun to find Charley Stoddard standing not ten feet away from him, rifle to his shoulder. *Damn all!* Ken thought, cursing himself for not remaining alert, not remembering that there had been three outlaws down there.

Ken Wingate rolled on to his back and triggered off his rifle at nearly the exact moment that Charley Stoddard fired his own Winchester. Wingate said something that was indistinguishable around the blood that filled his mouth. Charley Stoddard, who had dropped his rifle, pointed an accusing finger at Wingate as if to condemn him for some indiscretion or crime.

Then Charley Stoddard dropped to his knees. He shook his head, trying to clear the miasma behind his eyes and then fell pitched forward, his face landing against the boot of the already dead Ken Wingate.

On the rise behind the two dead combatants, Lee Saleen shook his head in angry wonder, rose and walked across the knoll to retrieve his horse. As he swung aboard, he wondered again at the lengths men will go to trying to capture a prize. Not nobly, but with cold avarice, destroying their own lives in the driven, perverted quest for wealth.

9

'That's it,' Jack Corrigan said to his son when the gunfire abruptly ceased. 'Ken got them.'

'We can't be sure,' Tabor said as Jack started to rise from his position of concealment. He had placed his hand on his father's sleeve, but Big Jack shook it away.

'Ken Wingate doesn't miss,' Corrigan said, standing to look down across the narrow road below. Tabor nodded. He wanted to argue for caution, but Big Jack could not be argued out of anything, and Tabor did not wish to appear a coward in his father's eyes.

'What do we do?' Tabor asked, removing his hat to wipe back his red hair.

'Make sure we have the evidence we need for the bounty! What else?' Jack asked.

Tabor flinched inwardly. He had heard the tales. He knew what sort of *evidence* Jack Corrigan would be wishing to take back to Adobe Falls. 'I don't know if I can . . . ' he murmured.

Jack Corrigan laughed roughly. 'Don't worry about it, Tabor. If it makes you queasy, Ken and I will take care of it.'

The sun was beginning to heel slowly over toward the west. Shadows had begun to creep out from the foot of the stack of boulders. Still the rocks retained all the heat of the torrid day, burning fingers and palms as the two bounty hunters clambered down to the road below and approached the granite bench.

'Wonder where Ken is?' Tabor asked, squinting toward the rise where the pinons grew carelessly, neglected by nature.

'Gathering his horse, I imagine. He'll be here. Come on, Tabor!'

Tabor Corrigan had an unsettling vision of his father taking his trophies, perhaps hanging them on his wall at home like mounted game animals. Shaking that bleak image off, he plodded along behind Big Jack, their boots stirring up tiny puffs of fine dust.

Crouching down they circled the ten-foot high granite monolith. Tabor's hands gripped his rifle tightly. He saw the twelve-inch Bowie knife at the back of his father's belt, the folded burlap bag thrust into the pocket of his jeans, heard a covey of desert quail on the slope beyond. Carefully rounding the corner of the bench they saw the two men, soaked with blood, lying still against the earth.

'I told you Ken doesn't miss!' Jack Corrigan said, and he set his rifle aside to step toward the bodies, unsheathing his knife. Tabor watched numbly. The sheerest of pale clouds drifted past them on the heated desert wind currents. A blue jay spoke harshly from the woods beyond.

Pearly Gillis sat up, his head lolling and shot Jack Corrigan.

'You rotten bastard,' Pearly panted.

'Why couldn't you leave well enough . . . '

Jack, stumbling back, holding his thigh with one hand, was nevertheless able to draw his Colt and shoot Pearly Gillis before the outlaw's final words could be spoken. Pearly, his head bowed, let his handgun fall free of his lifeless fingers and pitched forward to lie unmoving beside the body of Cody Minor.

Jack Corrigan was clenching his wounded leg with both hands now. He sagged to the earth himself and tore the scarf from his neck to bind his thigh wound with a rough tourniquet. He turned his brutal eyes toward his son.

'Why weren't you watching him, damnit!' Jack demanded.

'Dad, I didn't . . . '

'They were right — Ken and Luke Skaggs,' Jack said, tying his bandanna as tightly as he could as the dark blood continued to flow freely, staining his pantleg. 'They were right! They told me I was crazy to take you on a bounty. I thought I could make a man out of you,' Jack said viciously. 'I was wrong.'

Tabor felt hot disappointment well in his eyes. Pleadingly he asked, 'What can I do, Dad . . . Jack?'

'Find Ken, damnit! At least he's useful when the chips are down.'

Frustrated, angry, ashamed, Tabor spun on his heel and started making his way up toward the dark stand of trees.

He came upon the pony almost immediately. The animal's dark eyes watched Tabor's approach with dumb expectation. It had been standing without forage or water throughout most of the day, tethered to a pine bough. But it was not Ken Wingate's horse. The gray horse must have belonged to one of the outlaws. Tabor's heartbeat began to rise again as he studied the deep forest, watching for any sign of movement. How much more of this could he be expected to take?

Still, they would need horses if he and Jack were to be able to travel, and so he untied the gray and led it

174

carefully forward. He had not gone a dozen steps when a second horse whickered from a hidden copse and the gray answered it.

Another rider! Tabor hobbled forward, his knees weak, his heart sinking. Before he reached the second horse he came across the two dead men.

Ken Wingate lay sprawled across the earth and the outlaw his father had identified as Charley Stoddard was stretched out in close proximity. Ken's eyes were open. Dust had drifted into them.

Holding the gray horse's reins, Tabor Corrigan sagged to the ground. Everyone was dead or dying. All of them! He couldn't find the strength to go on. For long minutes he sat there, watching two silver squirrels cavort in the tree branches, unconcerned with human activities. Then the real or imagined sound of his father's voice commanding him to rise, be a man, continue on, brought Tabor slowly to his feet and he wove his way up the slope to discover

Ken Wingate's pony tethered there.

Untying it as well, he wearily began leading the two horses back down the hillside to where his father waited.

The shadows were spreading rapidly now, the sun a huge red ball above the broken western hills when Tabor reached Big Jack again. Corrigan sat watching grimly, holding his bloody thigh as Tabor walked the two ponies in.

'They got Ken, then?' Jack said, looking at Wingate's gray pony. Tabor could only nod, and his father asked for no details of the bounty hunter's death.

'All right, then,' Jack Corrigan said, rising with the assistance of his rifle stock and the granite bluff behind him. He peered into the darkening skies and muttered, 'Let's get moving while we've still got some daylight left.'

'Moving?' Tabor asked numbly. He kept his eyes averted from the two dead men nearby.

'That's what I said!' Jack Corrigan

said, his angry mood darkened, intensified by the pain in his leg. 'We're on a bounty. We finish the job.'

'But . . .' Tabor motioned toward the dead outlaws. 'We've done it, Jack.'

'There's one of them left, isn't there? The kid. The one called 'Billy'. I don't leave my work half done, Tabor.'

'We don't even know where he is,' Tabor complained, drawing another look of contempt from his father.

'We know where he has to be,' Jack answered, looking eastward. 'The ranch house. Probably holed up watching the loot. Or protecting the girl. You remember her, don't you?' Jack said, swinging awkwardly into the saddle, a bulging burlap bag in his hands. 'Oh, yes — he's there. The last man. He won't get away, I promise you.'

*   *   *

Through the last purple glow of twilight, Lee Saleen trailed after the two bounty hunters. They rode slowly, he saw, and Big Jack Corrigan was swaying heavily in the saddle. From time to time the younger man stretched out a hand to brace Jack. They were now heading toward the cabin where Cody Minor had had his hideout. What awaited them there, Saleen could not predict. He knew that the man who had fled the battle earlier had ridden there, knew that he had heard one shot from within the confines of the stone house. Who had fired, who might have been shot was only a guess.

Dusk faded to night and the stars began to blink one by one. A broad-winged owl swooped low overhead. From somewhere frogs began to chorus although there was no known water source nearby. But then, Saleen considered, the frogs did not need much water to survive. The stubby buckskin horse moved easily under him, although Lee could tell the animal was weary of the long trail. As was Lee himself. There was a light showing in the narrow window of the stone house and Lee wondered who awaited them, what bloody surprises the falling night might conceal.

★ ★ ★

'I heard something,' Virgil Spangler said, rising from the long plank table. 'Turn that lantern wick down!'

'I need the light to see by,' Vida Minor answered. 'I've a wounded man to tend to.'

'He won't make it anyway,' Virgil said dispassionately, glancing at Vida who sat near the still form of Billy Gillis. She had a tin basin of warm water on her lap, a clean cloth in her hand. At her feet a few bloody bandages were strewn. Billy had not moved for an hour, nor opened his eyes since Virgil, in his rage, had shot the young man. It was difficult to tell what Vida was thinking as she cared for the bare-chested man now inert on the cot where Woodrow Skyler had died. Virgil did not particularly care what she was thinking, nor if Billy lived or died.

'I'll do it myself,' Virgil said, shoving away his plate of leftover bacon and beans, all of the cooked food that Alicia had left behind. He strode across the room to the end table where the lantern burned and turned it down so that it gave off no more light than a dozen fireflies in a Mason jar. Then he bent and peered out through the window, his hand on the butt of his Colt revolver.

'Finish up what you're doing,' he snapped at Vida. 'Come full dark we're riding out, you and me.'

'He can't take care of himself,' Vida objected. Virgil Spangler glanced again at Billy Gillis and shrugged.

'Too bad. He shouldn't have crossed my path. Do like I tell you — throw a few clothes into a bag and change into a riding outfit. You're going with me, woman. One way or the other. Do you understand me, Vida?'

'Why do you want someone who doesn't want you!' Vida said, placing the bloody water pan aside.

'You really don't know?' Virgil seemed genuinely surprised. 'I'll show you along the trail . . . once we get out of here. Now,' he said, peering out the window again, 'I'm going to saddle two horses for us. Gather your belongings.'

Putting on his hat, Virgil cautiously opened the ranch house door and stepped out into the warm gloom of night.

Jack Corrigan shot him before Virgil even reached the hard-packed yard.

Virgil Spangler slapped at his pistol, clawed it from its holster and fired back even as he fell, aiming at the muzzle flash of Jack Corrigan's colt. The bullet whined off the metal of Jack's pistol and found flesh. The fragmented lead tore at Jack Corrigan's body and he sagged to his knees before he rolled over on to his side, blood filling his mouth. The life had gone out of Virgil Spangler before he buckled to the ground, but his bullet had done its work. Tabor Corrigan let out an involuntary moan, glanced at the dead outlaw and then knelt beside his father.

'Forgot there was another of 'em,' Jack Corrigan said hoarsely. He lifted his head and gripped Tabor's shirt front. 'Don't you ever do that, Tabor. Don't make the mistake I did.'

'I won't, Dad,' Tabor said. He looked briefly to the high, piercing light of the stars. They blurred in his vision. His father had let go of his shirt; now Big Jack looked up through his pain and spoke again.

'One left. Only one . . . the kid, the one they call 'Billy'. Get him for me . . . ' A terrible cough racked Jack's body and more dark blood flowed from his mouth. 'We get them all . . . when we take on a bounty, we get them all! Finish the job, Tabor. For me.'

Then Jack's head lolled back and he was still. Tabor Corrigan looked toward the open door of the ranch house and he rose heavily, cocking his pistol as he approached.

10

The room was dim as Tabor entered. By the flickering lamplight he could make out a forlorn woman sitting at a long plank table, articles of clothing scattered about her on the floor. And a bandaged, shirtless man lying motionless on a thin cot in the corner near the fireplace. As the hatless red-headed youth entered the room, Vida sprang to her feet and demanded:

'Who are you? What are you doing here?'

'Just get out of the way. I've a job to finish,' Tabor answered. He still had not found his father's authoritative tone and his voice quavered a little even as he lifted the muzzle of his pistol and shifted it to the man on the cot.

'This is my home!' Vida shouted. 'Get out of here. Can't you see we've got a wounded man here?'

'I see him,' Tabor said, his throat feeling dry and constricted. 'I mean to make it a lot worse.'

Neither of them heard the quiet approach of the tall man behind Tabor Corrigan, but the ratcheting of his pistol as he thumbed the hammer back was clear and unmistakable. Tabor glanced across his shoulder and smiled thinly.

'Richard Sly. So you are one of them after all.'

'No. My name is Lee Saleen. I'm a deputy United States marshal. Toss your iron away, Tabor.'

'Like hell I will!' Tabor shot back. 'The man on that cot is a bank robber named Billy.'

'And?' Saleen asked.

'And I promised my father . . . as he lay dying, that I would finish him off. He's wanted dead or alive!'

'He's alive now,' Saleen said. He had not moved from the doorway. 'Do you think he's going to put up a struggle if you try to take him in?'

Tabor hesitated. 'Show me a badge, Saleen. If you've got one.'

'I don't carry one out here. That's a good way to get shot by hotheads. And fools,' he said with emphasis.

'Then back off!' Tabor shouted with frustrated anger. 'I owe this to my father! I owe it to him to . . .'

'To end up like he did?' Lee Saleen asked quietly. 'To wander the wastelands killing indiscriminately? What's in that burlap bag hanging from your father's saddle, Tabor? Something you'd be proud to ride back to civilization with?'

'You don't understand!'

'More than you do,' Saleen said, shifting slightly to one side of the doorway. Tabor still had not lowered his gun. Vida still had not moved from her defensive position in front of Billy Gillis. 'I told you that my name is Lee Saleen. I can prove it to you back in Adobe Falls if you're willing to ride there with me.'

'And leave this bandit . . .' Tabor

erupted, gesturing at Billy.

'I told you that you don't know what you're doing,' Lee said forcefully. His eyes met Vida's across the darkened room. 'This man is known to me. His name is Ben Minor!'

'It can't be!' Tabor said, unnerved now and confused. 'My father told me . . . '

'And your father was always right?' Lee asked quietly. He waited and watched, and slowly Tabor lowered his pistol and ran a distracted hand across his forehead.

'I'm not a killer,' Tabor Corrigan told them all in a hushed voice.

The scrabbling, slithering sound on the porch didn't register until Saleen spun to see Big Jack Corrigan, covered in blood, clawing his way toward them.

'I knew I couldn't trust it to you!' the apparition roared. 'I knew you were always going to be a coward, Tabor. Get out of my way and give me a clear shot!'

From his elbows, Jack Corrigan

aimed his handgun at the cot where Billy Gillis lay, and Lee Saleen shot him.

Lee shifted his sights to Tabor, but the redhead seemed to shrink and deflate before their eyes. 'I'm done, Saleen,' he said. Then his pistol dropped from his fingers to clatter against the floor. Tabor did not glance at his father's body. He walked heavily to the plank table and seated himself on one of the benches, lowering his forehead to his knuckled fists.

The room was utterly silent for a minute until the weakened voice from the cot whispered: 'What is it, Vida? I thought I heard shots. Is the fighting over now?'

Vida Minor sat at the chair by the head of Billy's cot and rested her hand on his forehead. 'Yes,' she told the injured man, 'the fighting is over, dear. Go back to sleep. Get your rest; you'll be needing it for the long trail.'

After Tabor had gone, a haunted and lost young man, Vida turned the lamp up once more, boiled coffee and sat across from Lee Saleen, her attention only now and then straying from Billy Gillis.

'You two will be traveling on now?' Lee asked as he sipped at his coffee.

'Yes. Somewhere,' Vida answered with a shadow of a smile. 'Will he be in any trouble still?'

Lee hesitated and then shook his head. 'No. He was just young and reckless.'

'Like Tabor Corrigan?' Vida suggested.

'They were very alike, I suppose.'

'I felt sorry for Tabor even when he wanted to kill us!' Vida said.

'It can't have been easy for him — trying to live up to Jack Corrigan's twisted expectations.'

'No. I suppose no one will ever find that stolen money now, will they?'

'No, I don't see how.'

'Then it was all for nothing, wasn't it?'

They were silent then. The lantern

light flickered across the stone walls. Billy rested peacefully. Vida shifted her eyes to Lee's and asked, 'What will you do now, Saleen?'

'Me?' Lee asked with some surprise. 'What I've always done.'

'Hunting men?' Vida said. 'Is that all you have, Saleen?'

'I've a woman down in Waco who might think of me now and again,' Lee said, staring into his coffee cup. He shrugged. 'But this is what I do, Vida. I hunt men. It's my profession.'

'My brother, Cody, he called what he did his profession — robbing people,' Vida commented. 'Jack Corrigan, what he did — he called that his profession. Lee Saleen, I don't like that sort of profession. I'll tell you this!' she said with a little bit of heat as she again glanced toward Billy Gillis. 'He is never again going to get tangled up with men who need their guns as a part of their profession.'

'That's as it should be, Vida. I know he'll mend his ways; I know you're woman enough to make sure he goes straight. The two of you are young enough to start a new life away from the guns, away from the blood and violence.'

'But you, Lee Saleen!' Vida asked with soft concern. 'What about you? What will you do?'

Lee laughed and pushed his coffee cup aside. Reaching for his hat, he told her: 'As for me, Vida — I am going to continue to go about my job. Doing my best to make sure that men who use guns in their profession are punished for it.'

★   ★   ★

The night was warm and dry, but the pony Lee Saleen was riding seemed eager to be away from this killing place, and so, too, was Lee. He tugged his hat low and started the weary buckskin horse down the long trail. He glanced only infrequently at the star-filled skies, and not once back at the ranch house where a single lamp glowed in the window.

We do hope that you have enjoyed reading this large print book.

Did you know that all of our titles are available for purchase?

We publish a wide range of high quality large print books including:
Romances, Mysteries, Classics
General Fiction
Non Fiction and Westerns

Special interest titles available in large print are:
The Little Oxford Dictionary
Music Book, Song Book
Hymn Book, Service Book

Also available from us courtesy of Oxford University Press:
Young Readers' Dictionary
(large print edition)
Young Readers' Thesaurus
(large print edition)

For further information or a free brochure, please contact us at:
Ulverscroft Large Print Books Ltd.,
The Green, Bradgate Road, Anstey,
Leicester, LE7 7FU, England.
Tel: (00 44) **0116 236 4325**
Fax: (00 44) **0116 234 0205**

BLUEGRASS BOUNTY

Jack Reason

The most wanted gunman and outlaw this side of the Rockies, Jude Lovell, is about to hang in the town of Saracen. The crowds flock to be at the event of the century. But Marshal Brand is deeply suspicious. Why are there so many of Lovell's gang gathered in the town? Have they come to mourn, or to stage a daring rescue? When the awful truth dawns it wreaks a devastating toll of death and destruction.

KNIFE EDGE

Tyler Hatch

Brad Winters, ramrod of the Block F ranch, only wants to do his job. However, his boss Matt Farrell has other ideas: he wants to re-enact the Battle of Hashknife Ridge, which had been fought there fifteen years earlier. It means a meeting of North and South — and old hatreds are far from buried. Before the battle begins there are shootings, robberies and assassination attempts. And by the time it's over, the wonder is that there is anybody left alive.